Murder At The Lighthouse

Also by Beatone Hajong

A Turn in the Road
Side by Side

Murder At The Lighthouse

A Novel

BEATONE HAJONG

First published by NU VOICE PRESS 2024
An imprint of Hubhawks Pvt. Ltd
www.nuvoicepress.com

This is a work of fiction. Space and time have been rearranged to suit the convenience of the book. Except for public figures, hotels, and institution names, any resemblance to persons living or dead or the real events are purely coincidental. The opinions expressed in the book are those of the characters, and should not be confused with that of the Author.

ISBN: 978-81-970218-9-3

Typeset by Saanvi Graphics, Noida

Printed at Nutech Print Services - India

Published by Nu Voice Press

Dear Reader,

Sometimes, it's hard to narrate a story. This story was such kind to me. I had to go through lots of hard days and mental blocks to accomplish what it looks like today. In the many years of my life, I always had a thought to write a book or to become a writer. However, things have always stumbled and failed many times in the process. Never had I thought I could one day finish it and bring it forth to you. Similarly, this story projects the life of a detective who gets appointed for a case to be solved. Her ambition to become the best detective officer remains in the small cage of her longing dreams which unfurl when the murder of a Statesman takes place.

Thank you so much for the support, and for taking the time from your busy schedule to read this novel. It means a lot to me.

My Best,
Beatone Hajong

Contents

CHAPTER ONE

Getaway from Brooklyn

When the first plunge of the sharp-edged knife pierces his hairy chest, she thinks of her mother. The infamous Statesman lay dead as hell on a king-size bed, blood oozing from his body and spreading across the white velvet sheet. It had been a hell of a fight to kill the man. "May his soul rest in hell but not in Valhalla," she whispers in silence as she hurries to flee the scene. The subway is the easiest escape route. Her footfalls echo through the deserted station. She waits impetuously, panting steadily. The last train decelerates, empty and unoccupied. She knows it would wait for thirty seconds. The tunnel lights flicker, casting an eerie glow on the deserted subway station. She stands very close, alone, with a frightful demeanor. Daisy Collins scans the area, twitching in different directions as though to make sure no one is watching her. Behind her, meters away, a wall clock ticks eleven p.m., its size dwarfing her. She thinks very hard and rigidly about her present, but it yields nothing. The door smoothly opens up for her. She stands a few feet away from the door, her strides hesitating to follow. *One..two..three..* she counts. Soaked in blood, her stained clothes evince a terrible deed. She can still feel the grip of the knife in her hand. Infact, she doesn't feel guilty about what she has done in the past hour. On a count of twenty-nine, she steps in as her courage assembles. She thinks she did right and assures herself, despite knowing the police would be soon after her. The man deserved it, she persuades herself, this time in firm conviction.

She watches through the glass windows and prays for no one to follow her inside. She scrutinizes the room, scans every corner, remembers every bit of her presence, and finds herself master of the crime. She feels safe for not leaving any clue or evidence to follow her. She reassures herself repeatedly and makes herself believe she will never be caught. She sits quietly and waits for her destination. She watches the tunnel lights flickering on the speeding train, which scares her. In her mind, she schemes her next intent. Probably, she can go home directly. But even as she sits in silence, her nerves fray with each passing moment. When the train finally reaches Brooklyn and the doors slide open, Daisy hesitates. She inspects thoroughly before she exposes herself. Her heart races; she hears voices and whispers arrive from several directions. She can feel the cascade of fears assembling in her. In a haste of urgency, Daisy hurtles and races in time to a safer place, the ladies' room; whispers seem to follow her. She waits, holds up, and locks herself in. She hears the diminishing sound of the train passing away, the vibration ripples through. Minutes later, the station stands in silence, deserted, and none to wait.

Daisy gazes at herself in the rectangular, silvery, huge, shining mirror. She can perceive the mirror image and sense her inner reflection. The figure appears fearful under the intense glint. She steps back away from the mirror.

"What have I done?" she wonders.

No one is there to listen to her. Hastily, she washes her blood-stained hands. The water blends with the blood of the man, turning from colorless to red as it swirls down the sink. She avoids looking at her reflection in the mirror. When she is done, she takes a deep breath. She moves slowly and cautiously, taking one step at a time, trying to make no sound. Not even a trace of sound she wants to pervade. She unlocks the door and peers in both directions to avoid any human presence. Finding no one, she proceeds, escaping from danger. She unshackles herself and heads home. Daisy is tired and hungry. The sooner she escapes from the site, the better. She lifts her stained gown above her knee and races along the pavement. She uses dark patches, shadows, and silhouettes to hide herself, masking her identity. She speeds up faster than she has ever run before. Her head constantly twitches in both directions. She feels a twinge of fear when a voice passes by, and she hides herself in the dark. Yards away, she discerns the shape of her building, its shadow covering the pavement. She waits for the voices to pass, and then resumes her way. She sees her dark apartment across the street. This time, she doesn't wait but hurries to cross. She makes it safely without being noticed. Daisy breathes, then unclasps her tightly held gown, feeling the heaviness of the wet cloth.

"Thank God! I'm safe," she reads silently and confidently.

Just an hour ago, she was nearly naked and about to get fucked with the once respectable Statesman, Blanford Sky. Upon arriving at the hotel, she had already shaped her plan. It was a scheme for which she had long waited. Now, she reflects that there was no better way to handle the situation. She tries to avoid, circumvent, and entirely keep herself away from the events of the evening. Taking the long staircase to her apartment, she breathes as quietly as possible, striving to maintain absolute silence. She leaves no trace behind, not even her finger print on the railing.

Her footsteps are as soft as a turtle's, making not a single sound. Somehow, she manages to remain undetected. As the door opens up, it creaks, and she shuffles across the wooden floor. Inside the room, everything remains unchanged. She feels a wave of relief wash over her, reassured that she is home.

"The Statesman is dead," she thinks perfectly.

The lights illuminate her apartment, making it gleam. She avoids attending to anything else, quickly retreating to the bathroom. There, she undresses her gown, standing naked before the mirror. She finds no marks, cut, or scars anywhere on the body. Running her hand over her private part, she convinces herself that nothing has happened to her vulva. The man couldn't fuck her; she had wielded the knife before he had any chance. She feels at ease about it, then washes herself with hot water.

Daisy prepares dinner. The water boils at hundred degrees Celsius, filling the kitchen with steam. In a second, her soup will be ready. The kettle whistles. The clock ticks to midnight. The streets below are silent. The television keeps her occupied as she flips through channels, hoping none have reported the incident. She returns to the kitchen and pours her soup. The telephone rings once, twice, thrice. She initially dismisses it as background noise from the television. She takes to the couch, continuing to change channels. A minute later, the phone rings again. Daisy grows frightened. She switches off the television, feeling her spine shiver, her skin turn cold, and her heartbeat quicken. She dodges her mind, hoping the ringing will stop, but it persists, demanding a response. In the midst of silence, the telephone's sound shatters her courage. Her hands shake, trembling from head to toe. She picks up the receiver, its cold weight unnerves her. She hears a female voice but hesitates to put the phone in her ear. The voice continues, resonating. Finally, Daisy brings the receiver closer. Her voice is shaky, unsteady, and quivering with fear.

"Hello," she answers.

Daisy waits on the line, the voice vibrating in her eardrums. It's her mother, Leona Hill, calling from Long Island. She launches into a long list of complaints from the school director about Daisy's frequent absence from school. Daisy quietly watches the clock; the minute hand completes five rotations. She waits for her mother's voice to pause.

"Are you listening to me?" her mother asks.

"Yes," Daisy replies, though she has no idea what she has done in the past two hours, nor does she want to know what the director at school thinks of her.

"Mom, it's too late to talk. You should get back to sleep," she answered.

She drops the receiver and gets back to the couch, feeling perturbed by her situation. She spends another hour anxiously watching the news, but there is no mention of the incident. She recollects the hotel, the subway station, and her way home. She's definite that no one saw her, even when she was hiding in the dark. She persuades herself that she's safe from being caught.

At one a.m., her room goes dark. She tries to sleep but can't. The Statesman's murder plays over and over in her mind – the hotel, the red wine poured on her breast, sucked through her cleavage. The Statesman forced himself on her, trying to moisten her vulva, which she resisted. Being thrown on the bed, about to get fucked, left her profoundly daunted. Deep down, Daisy knows why she did that and why she took the risk. Suddenly, in the dark, she runs her hand over her private parts. She's still virgin, she assures herself. She shuts her eyes, lying still on the couch. The television continues in the background, but she hears nothing. She lowers the volume. The room flickers with the contrast and colors from the television reflecting on the walls. She avoids turning it off. Her effort continues in the dark, but she doesn't fall asleep, she can't. Her mind plays again and again. The fear occupies and petrifies her at the same time. It will haunt her for the next few weeks. She's sure of that. She thinks about her mother, knowing she can't share what she's done. It might overwhelm her mother or make her overprotective. Either way, the cage was open. Leona Hill once had an affair with the former Statesman – a short-lived romance that ended poorly.

Daisy had witnessed her mother's anguish over their breakup, now realizing it was ultimately for the best. However, Leona Hill remains unaware of what has happened to her former lover. She keeps calling her daughter once a week. This time it was the complaint message. Earlier, she did live with her daughter in Brooklyn, but after the breakup, she moved to her only property on Long Island, inherited from her mother. Anyway, it was her desire to change her dwelling. However, behind that desire, it's the inferior affair that went through in her apartment. The room which Daisy avoids now. She had seen her mother get exploited in her bedroom and heard her scream often when she was with Blanford Sky. Sometimes, he did try to force her mother. Daisy, haunted by her mother's suffering at the hands of Blanford, tirelessly schemed to liberate her. Witnessing her mother's nightly torment fueled Daisy's determination to act.

"Why don't you leave the man?" she once suggested.

"If I could break free, I would," her mother lamented.

Leona's inexplicable loyalty to Blanford Sky strikes Daisy as peculiar. It's the brief dream that jolts Daisy to the core, depicting her mother's vulnerability in bed. She can almost hear her cry, as Blanford hastily readies himself to depart, leaving her abandoned and silent in his wake.

Daisy awakens abruptly, her body perspiring. She glances towards her mother's bedroom in the darkness, calming herself with the reassurance that it was just a dream. Looking at the wall clock, she reads three a.m. before padding silently to the kitchen. Her thirst is quenched. The television is soundless, she behaves as a statue, steady on her couch, glaring at the screen. It doesn't interest her, puts it off. Then spends a while at the window. A stray dog briefly catches her eye before disappearing into the darkness. Her mind wanders back to her eighteenth birthday, marred by the absence of her friends and fuelled by anger towards the Statesman who kept exploiting her mother on a daily basis. She falls back on her couch, and a cool breeze fills the room, calming her thoughts. She lays down again. Contemplating her mother's tempting phone call, she resolves to visit her despite the uncertainty of what lies ahead. But what awaits at the break of dawn is unwritten in the script of her life. With determination, she prepares to escape the city, meticulously packing her belongings into a trunk, ensuring no trace is left behind.

Daisy doesn't miss anything as a clue to be left behind. Under the cover of dawn, she loads her stuff in a trunk, avoiding detection as she navigates through the silent city streets. Waiting for a ride, she feels the weight of her burden but remains vigilant, concealing her actions from prying eyes. She succeeds in moving silently until her feet touches the pavement. She inspects her perimeter and finds no onlookers, a small relief after her exhaustive efforts. As dawn lingers on the horizon, impatience drives her forward. In seconds, she finds the first light gleaming out to the east. Her impatient trait compels her to take action. She pulls her heavy trunk, scratching through the pavement that she isn't aware of. She hates the stupid noise from the edges of the steel trunk. She finds the mark impressed on the solid turf. She halts, moving no further. She doesn't want to leave any hints. Her face hoods in horror, panicking about the whole situation. She sees morning runners now. They pass without their eyes focusing on her. She's still unseen. But, she can see the waste-bin that she used to hide the other night across the street. Daisy quickly obscures her face with her scarf and adjusts her attire, the crimson hue of her top vibrant against the daylight. Then she straightens her dress and dons a white-brimmed hat, tying her scarf securely under her chin. Waving at a passing carriage, she raises her voice. It stops instantly.

"Take me to the rail station," she shouts.

She tries to appear as ordinary as possible. She suppresses her inner turmoil by focusing on the task at hand, escaping unnoticed. The coachman assists her in putting her trunk in the carriage. She settles and sits well, her stillness betraying none of her anxieties. As the carriage sets off, she breathes. She remains vigilant, and her eyes keenly observe each passerby. The aroma of freshly baked flatbread wafting through the chimneys teases her hunger, which she dares not satisfy. She's focused on leaving the city as swiftly as possible.

At the rail station, she applies herself to pull the trunk. She feels exhausted and thirsty. She remembers her flask inside her trunk. She fills it in half and moves forward to find her chamber. She can't see any tunnel ahead or light flickering. She's not afraid, she reminds again. She has done nothing, she convinces again. She's simply going on a holiday to visit her mother. Despite the absence of visible tunnels or flickering lights, she reassures herself that there is nothing to fear, repeating her fabricated story of visiting her mother as she navigates through the growing crowd. She can hear the buzzing crowds grow in a while. The clock strikes six. She prepares steadily and looks up at the rising sun in the east. She can forget everything in her last twenty-four hours, barring the crucial juncture at the *Hotel Grande Albergo delle Palme*. It lingers in her mind, a secret she guards closely as she leaves Brooklyn behind for good, lost in her contemplations.

CHAPTER TWO

Hotel Grande Albergo delle Palme

Detective Susan Kelly arrives five minutes late at the hotel. She is informed it is suite number thirteen on the fourth floor. The clock ticks five past nine in the morning as she stomps out of the elevator. She can hear voices and whispers and can see people and equipments. The yellow tape barricades the outside entry. She can see the New York State Police Department stamp on the yellow line tape.

"What took you so long?" inquires Corporal Tony.

"It's the Manhattan jam."

Corporal Tony, the man of precision, time, and accuracy, expects the best from whomever is under him. Over his span of forty-five-year career as a detective, he has never failed to uncover and resolve every case. Known for his perfectionist approach and tempered mind, he became famous as one of the top homicide detectives in the City. It was the probe of a Catholic Priest murdered by poison during Easter lunch, and he was the only person who could crack the case. The New York Times labelled him the number one homicide detective. Since then he has held that position with pride and honor. But, a hunch of delusion overpowers him as he approaches the hotel. It's the unusual scene at the crime spot that startles him. He then directs Susan for the examination.

She wades in his direction and takes up the charge, followed by few of her teammates.

"Is he always the annoying man in the group?" Susan murmurs to her co-workers.

"He wears his pride in his suit. He's the number one homicide detective. Don't dare to question his integrity. He will fire you," says one of her associates.

Susan sighs and breathes, "I can see that," an expression of weariness crossing her face.

She scans her eyes around the room. The forensic team had already done their first round of evidence collection. She shuffles toward the window, taps her feet, and gazes below. She can acutely smell aromatic wine on the bed sheet. She wants to do her best. It's her first case since she moved to New York. Young and radiant, in the late twenties, she is unmarried and single.

"It's quite a heck of a mess," she wondered.

She gazes at Corporal Tony from her spot. She expects a comment from him. Corporal Tony watches the team inspect the entire suite.

"There's nothing so concrete as evidence," Tony remarks.

"I can see the hard days ahead," replies Susan.

"You must take charge of it. I need every minute detail to be recorded. Make a comprehensive report."

"Yes, Corporal, I will do my best," Susan answers with conviction.

Tony prepares to leave. Blanford Sky's corpse was already wrapped in a body bag, awaiting transport. She's unaware of the victim and has not seen the face of the corpse.

"What's the name?" Susan inquires.

"Blanford Sky, a former Statesman, is approximately in his mid-forties," adds Tony.

"That's what politics does to men," Susan muses.

"I expect a good end."

"Sure," Susan agrees.

Detective Susan watches him cross the yellow tape line, followed by a few of his men. She resumes her attempt to decipher the rest of the case. She gets closer to the bed, where she smells the wine and the mixed blend of color stains on the bed sheet. It's blood. She takes a closer look at it and orders a hand lens. She examines well enough to find a clue. It's a strand of hair, notably long, indicating a female presence. With this discovery, she's now certain of a woman's involvement.

"You missed out on something important," Susan argues.

She hands it to the forensic team. The knife is still missing. She wades inside the bathroom. It's still wet, and the toiletries are cluttered. She looks at herself in the mirror and feels the privilege of solving the case. She leaves everything untouched and orders them to take charge of the fallen things inside the room. She examines the floor. Faded footprints are visible on crystalline marble. A slight hint of blood outlines the shape of the feet. Not one or two, it's a series of steps following out of the door. The runaway escape, she pictures it. The team collects the evidence. Meanwhile, Susan directs the photographer not to miss a single corner of the suite.

"Any sign of sexual activity, condoms, panties, underwear?" Susan inquires.

"We found an empty Trojan packet," reported a member of the forensic team.

"Probably it's still stuck on his dick," says Susan.

The clock ticks ten. It's been nearly an hour since they began analyzing the crime spot. Susan peeks at her wrist watch and concludes everything has been done well. The other team moves out and the elevator slides down. She waits, and once again she wants to give a round to make sure nothing has been missed. She tries to imagine and rolls a tape in her mind. Her speculation suggests the Statesman was intending to rape the girl. Her feet carries her towards the bed, the wine adding to her disquiet. The significance of the wine eludes her; she struggles to discern its relevance. She entertains another line of thought, considering whether the man may have poured it on the girl before the attempt, or if she had been intoxicated. She moves toward the window and cranes her neck out. The sunlight gleams at her. She ends there and moves out of the suite. She advances toward the elevator.

"Seal the room until we have it resolved," she commands.

She directs the authority and glides down to the ground floor. She can hear a buzz outside at the entrance of the Grande Albergo delle Palme. Walking alongside her teammates, she inquires, "What's outside?"

"It's the reporters," her teammate responds.

"This is going to be a difficult conversation. Make sure no one gives any detail," she instructs firmly.

She waits in the lobby. A team member walks out to meet the mob. The reporters, journalists, and columnists ask questions, but none are convinced. Later, after hearing the man, they concede about it, yet the buzz wants to hear from the officer in charge. He returns.

"Is there anyone from the Wall Street Journal?" she asks.

"Yes, not one, but many. They want to hear from you," he replies.

"What the heck are they going to write about it? It isn't going to change their market value," she sips her coffee. "Let's depart."

Susan finds the cluster at the entrance, ready to project their questions at her. She gets caught in the middle of the buzz, with cameras surrounding her and microphones directed at her mouth. She begins to speak. A question pours from the New York Times; she doesn't give much detail, providing only the required information. She doesn't want to mess with it in the media file. The case has just begun. She walks to her car.

"What a mess," she whispers. She reads the name of the hotel before she moves out. The news has already followed out, the buzz clattering in the channels.

"It's a difficult name to remember, Grande Albergo delle Palme," she reads.

Her car sweeps off past the clusters in a minute toward the headquarters. She has to report to Corporal Tony about the progress. She's confident that she has done well and somewhere in her mind her expectation has a higher value. She remembers well how often she was excluded from significant cases back in Chicago. Once, she nearly missed her name in the Chicago Tribune where an officer was saved from being shot. Later, it was the officer whose name resonated across the city. The Chicago Tribune called him *The Brave Son*, entitled boldly. Susan knew it was she who saved *The Brave Son* from his death. Now she thinks it's her time to show her bravery. This case will give her more recognition in the department and bring laurels to the New York State Police. She doesn't want to repeat the same thing, so she shifted to New York. Her automobile halts. She cranes out of the car and looks at the strong foundation of the tall building. She feels blissful to be surrounded by those skyscrapers, and her office is at the top. It's the headquarters building that fascinates her. She can't wait to go inside.

On the thirteenth floor, Corporal Tony sips his coffee amidst piles of files that have accumulated over the entire day. He reads through them. Then he looks at his computer and browses folders after folders, going through unsolved ones. The 1992 bizarre case of a murdered American woman in Mexico catches him, compelling him firmly. He stays with that. The case never surfaced in the mainstream media, nor was it resolved completely. Lately, the investigation was suspended on the grounds of no evidence of the accused. They termed it an accident.

Susan waits, leaning her body over the door frame. She knocks thrice and manages to get the attention of the Corporal.

"Come in," says Tony.

She grabs the chair and glimpses at the cluttered table. She's not sure how to begin or where to start. All she finds is that she's framing her words inside her mind. Tony waits for her to break the silence while he settles his files.

"Why aren't you saying anything?" he finally prompts.

"There's a lead," Susan responds.

Tony's eyes widen. "What's the proof?"

"We found a hair on the bed where the murder occurred, as well as foot imprints on the floor."

"Ensure it's authentic," Tony instructs.

Susan gets up from the chair. "The forensic analysis will be in a matter of a few days," she says.

"Thank you for your early report," replied Tony.

Susan watches as the beam glides through the glass panes, the daylight fading away from her sight. Out of the window, she can view another skyscraper, the place where she has been working for a month. She's tired and exhilarated. Her friend, Massy Paul, owns a bar. By sunset, she decides to make a visit. She needs some time alone, away from her bustling schedule. She takes her usual seat along the counter. She orders the same drink in the flavor she prefers. The television is on. She raises her heavy head to watch the game. Massy comes up with the glass. She perceives a few faces inside, none familiar. She can't interpret their facial expressions.

"Why would a lady cop come into a bar in uniform?" Susan tries to convince herself, just like the rest, that she's a normal lady at the end of the day.

"You were great today on television," compliments Massy.

Susan sighs deeply. "The reporters never listen to anyone." She finishes her drink, waits for a while, then prepares to leave.

"You should find someone to take care of you," suggests Massy.

"You mean like a boyfriend," she chuckles.

Massy shrugs, offering a reassuring smile. Susan nods, her vision falling on the displaying racks as she tries to read the brands. She reads some, then glimpses at her wrist watch. It ticks at 7 p.m. For the last time, she finds the same number of people inside. In the last hour, none have entered or left. She declines another drink, feeling a sense of loneliness. She can't express that or share it with anyone else. Neither does she desire to squeeze out her personal life which to many may sound boring and dull. Once she had someone she loved so much. It never worked out, and she had to end it. Now her broken heart finds solace in the bar.

On numerous occasions, Massy spilled her keenness of knowing what went wrong in their relationship, but Susan always declined to narrate her sad story. Jaded by those questions, Susan finally decided to open up that evening. She narrated as if she felt no remorse of their past, her face barely exhibiting any emotion, projecting toughness and dreadfulness like a cop.

"He was cheating on me with a younger woman," Susan blurts, taking her last sip.

"I'm so sorry to hear that."

"You shouldn't be. That was a long time ago. I have moved on since then. I'm strong and tough now. I know how men are."

"Indeed, you do exhibit toughness," Massy acknowledges.

"I'm glad I have a friend who owns a bar," she remarks before departing.

"See you tomorrow," Massy's voice reaches Susan as she exits through the door.

Susan gazes from her open space, her apartment on the fifth floor, granting her wide access to the outside world. She leans on her balcony's steel railing and lights a cigarette. She can feel the smooth breeze. The city light glimmers from towers and streets. This is what she had dreamed of over the years – the life exactly as she once envisioned. She can get whatever she desires in New York. She's a hard working cop and rich, she believes it firmly. In a short span of time, she has established herself in the department, and now she's assigned a case. She feels the most fortunate of all. When her cigarette turns completely into ashes, she dials her mother in Chicago. She picks up in her timid voice, coarse and rough, and talks about her moving to New York. Besides, Susan Kelly ignores her mother's praise for the television appearance.

"You know it's just the media," she remarks.

"I'm so proud of you," her mother insists.

"It's just the job," she says. "I'm coming to visit you next weekend."

She hangs up the call and spends a few more minutes outside, watching the skyscrapers glow in the armies of light. At ten p.m., she heads inside, pours herself red wine, and comforts herself in front of the television. She can see herself in uniform on the screen. The case of the murdered Statesman has already gained a reputation in the city. A high profile, confidential, classified matter of supposed importance. She watches herself give comments on the issue, but nowhere in the conversation does she mention the name of the hotel. It's a hard name, she tells herself. She sips her wine and then finds a camera focused on the hotel building. She feels pleased, her memory didn't fail her. She can read the name. The place has begun to receive repute of its own, either in a good or bad way, depending on the case. Susan pours more wine into her glass and tries to recall the name. She whispers to herself about the mysterious case of Grande Albergo delle Palme. She's eager for the routine of the next day, excited and animated. Her confidence magnifies, ready to crack the case with her expertise.

"A terrible murder," she reassures carefully. Susan yawns. At eleven p.m., her lights go off.

CHAPTER THREE

Long Island

Daisy Collins feels weary and fatigued from her long journey home. In the past few hours, she has forgotten she has committed a crime. She doesn't want to remember it anymore. All she can hear is the rumbling sound of the train along its track. In the last few hours, she has worked hard to keep herself away, distancing herself from people. She's not willing to disclose any indication of a potential issue. She stays silent, quiet, and steady in her seat. Her mother doesn't even know she is arriving on the Island. All she can do is wait, watching through the window of her seat. She succeeds in getting a fresh breath and exhales it out, making her feel safer than before. She can hear the whistle sound like a forlorn call in the dark night. The brake hisses and screeches through the iron tracks as it slows down to stop. She prepares mentally. What worries her is the hefty trunk she has to carry. She can see the noon light fading in the sky. Her feet touch down on the platform as she applies her strength to pull her trunk. It's wheelless; she regrets it. Outside the station, she waits for a chauffeur. She settles her gown, tilts the brim hat on her head, and ties her scarf knot properly. Her crimson red top attracts the eye. She finds a car. She motions herself with the heavy trunk. She takes her seat behind and urges to move out. The chauffeur shifts the vehicle, transits the other passengers, and smooths past the crowd away from the station in a minute. Daisy senses the sunlight overhead, so she cranes her neck through the car window. The breeze touches her and she feels it sink through her skin. She recalls the last time she came to Long Island. She dwells on her thought, as her mother would take it by surprise. Although the other night she heard her complaints, she reaches home after forty-five minutes of driving. Her feet trudge through the cemented porch outside. She feels her arm heavy and exhausted. She manages to reach the gate. The open-front courtyard waits for her steps. She follows the stone path along the line. A stone wall surrounds the house from the right and the left. The newly painted white wooden fence at the entrance glimmers. Daisy presses the door bell. Once, twice, thrice. Then she hears a voice creak down from the upper floor of the house.

"I'm coming," her mother shouts.

At nine p.m., Leona Hill prepares supper on the table. She's joined by her daughter, who appears preoccupied and self-centered. Their tiny mini television set sits on the table and keeps their ears occupied with the song it plays. Daisy pulls out a chair and sits quietly. She says nothing, but before doing so, she changes the channel to a newscast. Her mother pours wine for herself and offers some to Daisy, who denies it and instead sips water from her glass. There's a long gulf of silence between them. Then the news bulletin abruptly surfaces. Daisy can see and hear the voices of the reporters outside the Grande Albergo delle Palme hotel. She waits and listens intently. The investigation has already begun. She clears her throat and wets her lips again. She starts to feel discomfort. She can see Susan Kelly in uniform, interpreting in her own way.

"Did you see that?" Leona asks.

Daisy chews the remaining food in her mouth. "He deserves that."

"Don't you dare say that again."

"Why do you still care about him?"

Leona feels remorseful about it, her pupils dilating as her eyes nearly fill with tears. She mourns silently for the man she once loved. She can't express how terrible she feels right now.

"Because he was a good man," she breaks down.

Daisy fails to comprehend and leaves the table. "No, he wasn't."

She retreats to her room, overwhelmed by fear. Her vision lingers for the long run, driven by earthly nightmares for which she isn't prepared. She's afraid now that she might be discovered by police personnel. She feels unsteady, taunted by the news of the murdered Statesman. She paces back and forth across the room. She can feel her legs shake and her hands quiver, trying as hard as possible to calm herself. She replays the entire scene again and again. This time she gets a narrow call, somewhere she can feel the fissures of her attempt. She decides to keep it secret, lingering in fear and horror. "Stand mighty," her demonic mind tells her. She breathes deeply after a prolonged altercation. A debate she chooses to accept. However, she's yet to perceive the intent of her mother toward the dead man. Why? Her feet slowly rise, one at a time, and she moves toward the window. It feels shuddering and compulsive to read and make sense of what she has been thinking over the past hour. She opens the window and feels the flurry of wind that brushes her skin with a cool sensation. Far north in her direction, she can observe distinctly the unrepaired pier, the stiff lighthouse painted white, and the concentrated beam stretching miles into the deep ocean. Memories flood back to her from days gone by. She feels her emotions burst into shattered glass – soft, fragile, and non-resilient.

Since the erstwhile Statesman entered their lives, Daisy and her mother had been in rough patches. They often fought with each other, sometimes barely speaking at dinner table. This would continue for weeks. Daisy blamed the man, while Leona admired him, leading to conflict and hatred between them. During her growing years, Daisy grew fond of her father, while Leona felt abandoned as she was left aside. The bond between Father and Daughter grew stronger over the years, whilst Leona Hill watched them from her porch every morning walking toward the Lighthouse. She felt the need for love and care from her husband, which she was deprived of for long. Nonetheless, she included Daisy Collins in her solitary prayers every night. Leona Hill loved her daughter as much as she began to hate her husband for drifting apart.

As a child, she tightly gripped her father's hand as they walked every morning to the lighthouse. Her tiny feet struggled with the steps. Her father lifted her on his shoulder from where she could see the distant water in miles. She sometimes used her father's binoculars to find dolphins swimming. In the evenings, she chose to be close to the water, waiting for her father to come down from the top. She waited for him along the pier, searching for fish. Her fondness grew everyday and she never missed a single chance to be with him. During winters, she waited for the snow to cover the surroundings, made a snowman, hit her friends with snowballs, and spent entire days outside with her father. When the snow covered each and every corner of the town, the ocean remained still, static, silent, and unheard of its roar; the waves hit, lapping the shore at a low pace before retreating into the ocean. Then she came with her friends, made tea for her father, and spent the entire evening at the pier fishing with her mates. She was observed by the lightkeeper up from the top. She would proudly shout to him whenever she caught a fish. Her father would commend her skills and instruct, "Take it home. Let mamma cook."

"One more, papa!" she burst out in a high pitch.

She returned home with her group of friends at dusk. On her left she held the sling of fishes and on her right she carried a bucket of snow to sculpt a snowman for Christmas. She was happy and cheerful.

One summer night, her eyes erupted into a torrent of tasteless tears. She felt empty and less lively after crying for three hours. The stormy night was there to change their fate. Her father didn't return home. The ocean seemed rough, and the tides were cruel. The waves crashed on the shore, heavy and strong. The light keeper never returned home. While attempting to tie his boat, the swells showed no mercy. They crushed him, pulling him into the deep, and a lapping of water swirled around him. His throat was choked with the flow of water, and somewhere in the deep ocean, his soulless body drowned. The pier was broken, and the boat shattered. Its wreckage and debris were seen along the coast the next morning. The fatal summer continued for a long time, and the incident never faded away. Daisy still remembers it, fresh and aching.

"Dad," her feeble voice whispers.

Her hand rises, points in the direction of the apparition, and then disappears. The vision. She feels the fresh air stroke her hand, returning her to her senses. Had her dad been alive, they wouldn't have moved to New York. Blanford Sky wouldn't have died. She wouldn't have to kill the Statesman. And now, the police are after her, Daisy reckons.

At dawn, she strolls toward the lighthouse. Her footfalls are unheard, cautious of any noise. She takes the long walk along the coast and the sandy gravel. She feels the craggy pebbles and the loosely packed sand that are washed away by the waves at intervals. Up above her head, she hears the gulls squeak. She feels the ocean breeze periodically following her. Her sight enlarges as she draws closer to the white painted lighthouse. She walks past the broken pier, projecting a second glimpse. She can see no one, but she expects someone to take care of the place. She prepares to climb the steps to the top. Then she hears a voice that prohibits her.

"You aren't supposed to be here," he says, the new lighthouse keeper.

Daisy doesn't recognize him, but she is willing to talk to the man. He looks humble and kind, with a shovel on his right and a bucket of sand on his left.

"My father used to work here," she says.

The man realizes soon enough that she was the daughter of the previous keeper who died on the uneventful stormy night.

"I'm sorry for your tragic loss," he says.

She nods. "I live with my mother now."

Daisy points her index finger in that direction. The man can see the white picket fence and the stone walls from the distance.

"Are you the daughter of Mrs. Leona Hill?"

"Yes," she breathes. "How's winter here now?" she asks.

"We don't get enough snow now. It's short-lived."

After her father's death, she hadn't visited the small town. For her, everything seemed new, changed, and altered. She didn't even remember her childhood friends. She felt lonely at every stage of her life. And now she would be declared a convict. This discovery would be new, something she had been waiting for since she left Brooklyn. She held onto her thoughts, trying to cogitate the smallest details of her childhood days.

The man allows her to ascend to the top while he collects his shovel and bucket to fill a pit at the adjacent site. Each stride takes her into the past. She doesn't need help anymore. She misses her father's shoulder and feels the edges of the carved staircase. At the top, she waits for the natural beam of the sunrise in the east, feeling delightful as she watches. The stretching ocean is calm and steady, and the horizon glitters in yellow-orange, its edges sharp and shiny. The breeze grazes through her. For so long, she has abandoned this place.

"It feels like home," her heart resonates.

In this moment, she's not the person who fled Brooklyn; she's not the person who could be called a convict. She's simply the daughter of the late lighthouse keeper. She gazes at the far arc of the ocean's edge, envisioning her father's return from the water. She can't deal with it being real, but deep down she honestly prays for it to be him. She spends another few minutes with her sight shortening as the beam overlooks her. She descends and extends her gratitude to the man for allowing her.

Daisy allows herself to be enveloped in nature's enclosure. She doesn't pretend to fear what she has done. Her feet drag her to the pier where her footfalls creep on the wooden wharf. The harbor isn't the same anymore. There are a few boats at the site. She stops at the waterfront at the end of the pier. The ripples are gentle and the lapping is smooth. She sits on the broken end of the dock, her legs hanging freely, tucked under the water. She feels the cold ravine of the water, a chasm she remembers from her childhood. Momentarily, she shudders. She can't stop thinking about the erstwhile Statesman. It flashes vividly – the blood dripping from his body, the number of stabs she pierced through his flesh.

"I had to do it, Dad," she weeps, knowing no one is nearby to see her. "I had to kill him for Mom," Daisy babbles.

She reassures herself. She doesn't need to be afraid anymore. Her moistened eyes dry out, and her legs play with the water before she embarks on her return. She makes a sloppy move. For the final time, she glances at the lighthouse. She sees the man at the top, fixed on his binoculars. Her feet wade again, following the same path – the loosely packed sands and the unshaped shiny gravels. From the farthest end of the ocean, the breeze traverses, winnowing across the coast. She finds peace. She cannot comprehend how she perceives her life now.

"It will never be the same," she laments. She looks at the vast ocean before she trudges off the coast. The beam remains alluring and bright as she observes the sun rising above the horizon.

Leona waits in the front yard. She feels the warmth draped over her arm in bright light. The memory refuses to leave her, finding space in her view and resonating in her vision – the affair she had with Blanford Sky. The truth seems hard to digest, indefinite, and unyielding from what she witnessed in the past few hours. She hesitates, failing to comprehend her affair with the man whose death remains a mystery for now. "It isn't my fault," she reminds herself again and again. Still, her doubts remain uncleared – who could have killed the Statesman? She assures herself that she won't be involved in any further affairs. Leona Hill waits for her daughter as she squints her eyes, watching Daisy approach from a distance with her shawl draped over her shoulder. Daisy can see her mother distinctly over the white-painted fence. Commotion dwindles in her mind as she prepares to open up to her. Though she was rude the other night, she also believes revealing the truth about the man's end is justified. Daisy arrives in the front yard, feeling reluctant toward her mother, unable to express herself better. She doesn't blink or make eye contact with her.

"Sorry about last night," Daisy finally says.

"You're right. He deserved it," Leona replies.

"You know the deal. I obeyed you."

Leona nods. She remembers the night when she promised to end, once and for all, everything that linked her with the Statesman. She has suffered – forced into sexual intercourse of no consent, beaten by the man – a long tormenting pain she endured, and her daughter has seen all of that. Nights were evil, days were cruel, and the man imposed on her. Burdened with pain and abuse, her intent was well read by her daughter. Lately, by collective decision, they framed their anecdote to deceive Blanford Sky. Daisy exhibited her courage that night and embarked on her mission – the errand she promised to fulfill. Blanford Sky, a rich former politician, falls into the lane of the luring drama, a story set to end his life.

"You're my daughter. I shall have you protected," Leona asserts.

"You never loved the man," Daisy says.

She flashes a self-satisfied smirk and glides inside. At the breakfast table, she waits for her mother. The drama ends, successfully accomplished. They are now rich and wealthy.

CHAPTER FOUR

The Protocol

Detective Susan Kelly decelerates her car. She glances outside, surveying her surroundings. She's aware of the massive building beside her. She quickly glances at her watch. She's ahead of schedule. She inhales deeply before stepping out. It's the view ahead. The newly decorated gesture and its appearance confound her. Over the week, Hotel Grande Albergo delle Palme received mixed reviews in the media and print. Susan sees the porcelain vase at the entrance, adorned with exotic plants. She gets the business out of it. She enters.

The lobby is, as anticipated, packed with newly arrived tourists, none with the idea of the murdered suite. It's supposed to be a secret, a classified finding. Susan hears French, Italian, and German at the same time. It is an odd prospect that she hears a British accent. She leaves the foyer, away from the Europeans, her footfalls reverberating. She's supposed to complete her protocol, collect footage from the operation rooms, and unlock suite number thirteen. She makes it quick, then navigates toward the fourth floor. The elevator door enlarges the space for her. She's followed by her men, two in departmental uniform. Suite number thirteen is the same as they had left it. In her second attempt, she thinks optimistically and listens to the chaos outside as her feet drag toward the window. She finds nothing new except the foul odor in the room. She dictates to seal again. She proceeds through the same hallway, then to the foyer. This time, the backpackers are gone. Susan peers around and then remarks on her assessment – a good deed.

"Nice makeover," she comments to the manager.

"I had no choice; it was all over the news," he replies.

"Keep it up. Make sure it doesn't disturb the tourists," she adds.

The manager watches her steady move. She flawlessly gets inside the car, puts on her sunglasses, and shields the window. The Chevy accelerates in the opposite direction against the honking of New York traffic. Susan gets a few photographs on her mobile phone of suite number thirteen to ensure that it doesn't confuse Tony, who has a reputation for being the forgetful brain in the department. He waits on his table impatiently, shuffles back and forth, then goes to the window. He sees the swarm of vehicles lined up, waiting for the green light. He reaches for his phone and dials the number.

"Where are you?" he asks.

"On my way. Stuck again," Susan replies.

"I can see that," Tony remarks.

She gets out of the car and moves a few paces ahead. It starts to get warmer, and the scorching hours will be prevalent soon. She hangs up her call and retrieves it. She can hear the honking, and the buzz gets messy. Intolerable and unbearable – the New York traffic. It's peak hour, the city reaches gridlock, all directions waiting for their release signals. She waits inside; in the meantime she fiddles with her phone, browsing through the pictures she has gathered from the hotel. She counts the number of cars ahead in the line, then locks her eyes on the red light. She feels trapped on both sides, the vehicles parked closely aside, even the long queue remarkably stretched out behind her, out of her eyesight.

"This is a ghostly city," she remarks.

"It can't get worse than this," says her teammate.

The green light shines. Susan feels at ease; her pupils shrink in the daylight. The automobile moves and turns right toward the headquarters. At ten, she finds herself entering the building. The elevator makes them wait. The team waits in the foyer. Meanwhile, the vehicles outside ease up moderately and green light flash from every street corner. The elevator bell snaps. Susan sees a rush of people coming out. They wait for them, then glide inside. Her finger reaches the button and presses it, and the thirteenth-floor lights up. It swiftly moves upward. Her mind echoes, stirred by the havoc, to find clues in the footage. She can't wait any longer. The door opens and she steps out, followed by her men. First thing, she needs to report to Tony. She remembers the urgent call. She knocks on the door, seizing his attention. Tony doesn't look up and is thoroughly engaged in his files. He hums, assuming the guest understands the welcome. He flips another page of the file before taking a break.

"What was the urgent call about?" asks Susan.

"Well," he frames his expression. "It's been resolved."

Susan looks at his cluttered table, wondering why the files are there.

"Are you reopening the 1992 case of a murdered American woman in Mexico?"

Tony gapes at her, not saying anything for now. "Did you get the footage?"

"Yes."

"Great, let's find the culprit," he says and gets off the table, heading out of the room. "1992, what a setback."

Susan follows him to the control room. She can see mammoth-sized screens displaying every corner of the building. It's her first time entering the room.

"This is quite the tech," she says.

Tony lingers at her surprise countenance. "You shouldn't be surprised; instead, feel fortunate about it."

She nods, then delivers the footage to the experts in control. The footage begins to play wide on the screen. The seriousness of the examination absorbs their eyes. Reserved and totally quiet, none speak, but the tape keeps rolling – at nine a.m., ten a.m., twelve p.m. But there's no clue or any sight of the murderer.

"Are you sure it's from the same day?" Tony asks.

"Yes, I'm sure about it. It's the entire day's footage, of course" affirms Susan.

"We need more to decipher. What about the forensic report?"

"We will get it by noon," she assures.

Susan follows Tony back to his workplace. He has those mysterious eyes that suggest serious foresight is guiding them. He sits in his chair and gestures for her to occupy the other. He demands for two coffee shortly after. Tony plays with his goatee, deeply engrossed in his internal musings. He turns his chair towards her. His mind vividly recalls the presence of a woman.

"You mentioned a woman."

Susan flutters her eyes, mulling over her comments on the case. She has no doubts about it. She drinks her coffee from the cup, her voice breaking slightly.

"We found her hair," she says.

"That alone won't tell us about the woman in the footage."

"Then we will have to wait for the forensic analysis," Susan replies.

He nods his head, sips his coffee, stands up, gazes out of the window, and then turns to face her.

"You've done a good job. You didn't miss any of the protocols."

Tony appreciates her. Susan strolls out of the room, bumping into her colleagues who have heard the recent rumor of appreciation. Susan tries to keep her composure, but she can't hide it when the entire department learns about it. She smiles at whoever she comes across before she slogs into her workplace. She gets a cup of coffee, turning her chair towards the window, craning her neck out, only to find the crowded street below. She hears the sound of horns and the cranks of heavy trucks. She's lazy and tired of the day. The coffee revives her, and she returns to her table. She places her wristwatch on it and glances at the time, then her finger rolls the mouse. The monitor blinks and flashes a file, a missing file long gone. She dwells on her interest and types the keyword. She reads the preliminary, having never heard about it in so many years of her service. She felt it was more like a crime fiction novel. She cannot forget the bizarre murder case of an American Woman in Mexico in 1992. Later, she discovers that there is a movie based on the story. Although Tony didn't validate that the case could likely be reopened, it's a standby as of now. She gets engrossed deeply in the moving story, which somehow gives her the little insights that she barely knew about.

"It's a bloody politicized mess," she remarks.

She carries a bag of conflicting thoughts, leisurely free from pressing business. All she waits for is the forensic report. She periodically checks her email, then replies to those she finds authentic. She reminds herself about the upcoming weekend;

she needs to bring her mother to the city. She waits for another hour, and so forth.

At three p.m., she looks out of the window. The automobiles are queued up, and she hears them honking in the congestion again. The sunlight leans away from the glass shield, slanting toward the west. Far in the distance, she sets her view atop a skyscraper, and a chopper swings away in the middle of Manhattan, fading away soon after. She's absorbed in the city sight. Predominantly, it's her broken heart cutting its edges into pieces. She still isn't over the relationship, though years have passed now. She pretends to be strong, like many others, counselling herself to get over it soon. She doesn't hear the knock at her door, engrossed in her thoughts. On her third attempt, she breaks free.

"Come in," she responds.

She hears the thud on her table. A bunch of files pile up next to her computer.

"The report," says the officer.

Susan reverts her interest; the officer leaves. She looks at each file individually, scanning meticulously, trying to employ her mind with every possible clue she can gather. She spends an hour neck-deep in work, then heads to Tony's office. She knocks, doesn't wait for the response, slides in, and places the report on his desk.

"She's an eighteen-year-old girl," says Susan in a convincing tone.

He doesn't seem to be convinced for a while, scrutinizing the report. He takes the report in his hand, looks at her, then remarks as he flips through the pages.

"Are you sure?"

She nods intently, persuasively. "Also, the killing took place around eight or ten p.m. Multiple stabs," she adds.

Tony goes through it earnestly, then suggests shifting to the operation room for the footage examination. He gets up from his chair and paces toward the operation room, with Susan following him.

"I want to see what this eighteen-year-old girl looks like," says Tony.

In the room, the CCTV footage is displayed on the screen. This time, they are more precise and confident in their findings.

"Roll from eight to ten p.m.," directs Tony.

Susan sharpens her eyesight in front of the brightly lit screen. She finds it difficult at some point to interpret the images. She steps back and allows others to read the screen. She stands a few steps away from the rest, leaning her back against a table, arm crossed. She watches Tony intently as he makes a remark.

"Hold it there."

Susan steps forward, intrigued and thrilled. She tries to watch closely.

"Damn, she looks so young!" she exclaims.

"That's her," confirms Tony.

Daisy Collins' face is captured on camera. Her face distinctly reveals her intention, wearing a gown unlike the others. Her straightened hair flares in the open air. She looks fearless, brimming with determination, with a fierce look on her face. She doesn't speak in the foyer but heads straight to the fourth floor, suite number thirteen. It's confirmed – Susan Kelly believes it's her. She spends a few more minutes studying the details, then walks out with Tony.

"Get every detail about this girl," Tony instructs.

She nods and returns to her table. She remembers the bar and prepares to leave, glancing at the clock – it's five p.m., with New York traffic lining up. The sun has gone down, and the fading beams have begun to change color. She doesn't want to miss meeting her friend, Massy Paul, at the bar. She drives through but gets stuck in the chaos of congestion. She feels trapped in the middle of the loud noise. Minutes pass until the green light finally allows her to speed up and cross a few blocks. She spots a parking space and parks quickly. In a rush, she enters the bar and is warmly welcomed by her dear friend. She takes a seat at the counter. She scans her eyes entirely, noticing some familiar faces. Next to her, a man in his thirties sits quietly, lost in his worldly dreams. He seems drunk but keeps sipping from his glass, not looking around.

"You seem a bit stressed out," Massy says, stretching out her arm.

"It's about an eighteen-year-old girl," Susan says, drinking from her glass.

"Care to share?"

"We caught her in the CCTV footage."

"An eighteen-year-old girl? That's not possible."

Susan's pupil dilates and grazes the light in the faintly lit surroundings.

"We've got evidence. She killed the Statesman," she says.

"That's unthinkable."

Susan taps the counter and asks for another drink. She doesn't want Massy to do that. She wants her company. The man next to her hears all of these things.

"You're the cop who's examining the case. She's deceiving you."

"Who are you?" questions Susan.

"I'm no one, but it's not her; it's a woman in her late thirties," he says.

The man gets up from the chair, thanks Massy, and walks out of the door.

"Do you know him?"

"He's a regular visitor."

"What did he mean by a woman in the late thirties?"

"Well, I'm not sure, but I feel he kind of knows something about the murder of Blanford Sky," Massy tightens her lips.

Susan clutches her glass and finishes her drink. She sounds curious about the man and intends to unravel all that she wants to know. She lingers on that and snaps again. She's unsettled and unnerved.

"Does he have a name?"

"He's Alan. That's all I know about him."

Massy is unsure of where this is going, but she feels Susan needs a hand to help her out of the bar right then. She sounds drunk and her footfalls are unsteady. Massy drops her off in the car.

"Are you sure you can drive?"

Susan belches. "I'm bringing my mother next weekend," she prattles.

"Good to know. You need to go home and rest."

She watches her, then twitches around to observe the automobiles on the road. Somewhere in the back of her mind, Massy fears about Susan. She doesn't stop her or ask her to wait. She's a cop; she can do it, and it reads her well. The car engine starts, the gear fixes, and the eyes are glued to the road. That's how Susan drives. The car pulls off the road in seconds, and the noise leaves a mark behind. Massy sees the car light ahead and Susan in the distance. She stares with a smile, then walks to her bar.

CHAPTER FIVE

The Sunday Prayer

Daisy wakes to the crowing of a rooster. The window brings the first shimmer of the beam. It opens to her vision the lighthouse. The air smells abruptly of wet dunes from the coast. She feels ticklish with her sensitive nose. She lays her feet on the wood flooring and hobbles toward it. Her sight searches for her mother in the front yard. She's already late, she checks the time. It's Sunday, she remembers, she's supposed to visit her father's grave. Instead, she's stuck within the white picket fence and the stone wall that surrounds her. The color radiates in intensity; she jolts on that. She can see her mother walk in, and the voice calls her instantly. To keep herself informed, she doesn't miss any updates about the investigation. She still believes she can't be traced, a convincing intuition.

"Hurry up."

"Just a minute, mom," Daisy responds to that.

She quickly pulls a towel and a robe from her closet. She's ready to shower before she gets out. Her footfall rams the floor, distinctively discernible to her mother down below. Leona Hill waits for her daughter at the breakfast table. Her preparation with the flowers modestly convinces her of the love she holds for her husband. First, she will go to the church and then to the cemetery, she maps it well for the day. Daisy stands in front of the mirror. Her wet hair drips water on the floor. She rinses with her towel. She uncovers herself, the robe falling on the wooden floor. She stands naked, feels her breasts, cups her palms and measures their size. She feels satisfied with what she measured; it's growing. It's getting bigger and turning into a woman's breast. Had she not killed the Statesman, the man would have touched her, she imagines. She fantasizes she's being fucked, her hand reaches her vulva, and clicks with her fingers over and over. She moans as if she can feel the other man's body rubbing on her. She rises, and her imagination unfurls. The pleasure continues.

The knock strikes hard at the door. The motion seems ceaseless. The longer it waits, the louder it gets. Then the voice erupts.

"Daisy."

The bang at the door wails harder. Daisy hears the interruption and then paces to get dressed. She wears jeans and a tank top.

"Coming."

Within a minute, she limps down to the breakfast table. She portrays her curiosity on her face and the day's timetable. Leona watches her closely as she serves her milk and toast.

"What took you so long?"

Daisy picks up the toast, smells around its edges, and applies the butter before she takes a bite and starts to munch. "I was reading the news. Anyway, what's the plan?"

"At first, we go to church, then the cemetery."

"Church? That wasn't even in the plan."

"Just hurry up," Leona says.

The breakfast table appears disorganized. It has nothing to do with the excess of stuff on the table. But they have a small kitchen, too small to fit a dining table in it. Somehow, it has continued for years. Daisy's mother waits outside in the front yard. She has done the cleaning of the truck, which she owns, since last summer. Meanwhile, the television set natters about subjects which don't appeal to Daisy. It's the news about the investigation that concerns her. She turns the knob and changes the channel, but there is no clue yet. She can hear her mother calling. She pulls the plug from the television set and hurries out.

"Are you going to drive?"

"Yes. You don't have your driver's license yet."

Daisy sits beside her mother and watches her switch gears. The road drives along the coast line. She grazes through her vision, the lighthouse, and the keeper who waves at them. She does the same. Up high above, she can hear the flutter of gulls from the sea toward the coast. She breathes in the fresh air.

"How did you find the new keeper?"

Daisy clears her throat, then ponders for a moment before turning to her mother. She falls short of description.

"He's kind."

She cranes her neck out of the truck window and looks back. They are out of sight of the lighthouse. Miles after, a few heads catch their sight. Leona parks the truck in the parking space. She hears the church bell toll, multiple times. Everybody goes inside. It's a small population inside, gathered for Sunday prayer. Daisy isn't sure if she wants to go inside and hear the whispers. She doesn't follow her mother immediately; instead, she chooses to stay outside. Unpleasant expressions surface on her face; she can feel and read them.

"Are you sure you don't want to do this?"

She nods at her mother, watching her walk in with the others. She counts the steps of the church one must take before entering.

Then she retreats into the open space where the vehicles are parked. She can't see the ocean or hear the gulls' cry. Her vision keenly observes the vast stretch of meadow, horses grazing on the highlands, and the blistering beams of the morning sun touching the ground. She enters into a mental conflict: how could a killer not be scared of entering a prayer hall? She tucks herself into the truck and waits for her mother. She decides she will not return to Brooklyn or attend school anymore, regardless of the director's complaints. It's over; she makes her mind firm. She's eighteen and can make her own decisions. The day brightens, but she sees no more people approaching. She twiddles with her phone and sends a message to her mother.

"Is it done yet?"

She gets no reply and grows impatient, turning up the music volume. She sees a bunch of flowers wrapped in velvet cloth. Sometime later, Leona Hill barges out of the church hall, curious and stunned by what she hears – the loud music. With urgency, she crosses the grassy ground. The truck door creaks, and the loud music evades into the empty space outside.

"What the hell are you doing? Turn that crap down right now!"

"You bored me," Daisy utters.

Leona takes charge of the steering. She settles into her seat and turns the key. The engine starts, roars, then shifts gear. Daisy feels uneasy, a twinge of guilt for texting her mother earlier.

"Where are the rest?"

Leona sifts through the flowers before she makes a move. She lapses again into the velvet clothing she has chosen. Daisy takes them from her, still waiting for an answer.

"They have a long ceremony," says Leona.

The truck pulls out of the place. Daisy holds the flowers in her hands.

"Dad would be happy to see us."

"You think so, after all that has happened."

She chooses to stay silent and wait. They take the same route along the coastline. The lapping of the water singular, the ripples crawl back into the deep. It's the silent affairs of the ocean, and the bright sunny day joins in. Daisy keeps following her gaze along the swells, finding none to wave at on the stretching path. Then the truck takes a left turn. The cemetery gate falls into their view. Leona stops. They walk in. A lone thought ruminates over her mind. Leona sees her daughter and the delight she holds for a short period of time. She doesn't know she has some truth to share that has left them behind. As they walk along the rows of headstones, a burial ceremony is in process.

"Was dad buried the same way?" Daisy inquires.

She doesn't remember. She had been a child when he was buried.

"Yes."

They halt in their steps. Daisy sees the name *Fritz Collins*. Her mother intends for her to offer the flowers. Her feet make a slow tread, feeling the dense, soft grass beneath her bare feet. She drops the flowers on the grave bed and returns to her mother a few feet away. Her hands clasp together, waiting silently. Leona mutters words as a sort of prayer, then urges her daughter to offer the same.

"Your father was a good man," she says.

"Do you miss him?"

She nods her head and walks. Leona apprehends the need to let her daughter know. She feels terrible about it, quite guilty, as if the truth always shadowed her.

"Your father knew him."

Daisy stands still momentarily. She finds it hard to digest the words. The blow of the truth hits her in many ways, leaving her indescribable. She tries hard to comprehend what she has just heard.

"Blanford Sky knew dad, and you didn't think it's important to let me know?" she yells.

"This is not what I wanted."

"Why did you make me do this?"

Daisy erupts into a volcanic flare; her eyes gleam with anger and hatred. She walks away violently, not listening to her mother.

"Because you knew what he was doing to me."

Leona sees her daughter slowing down. Daisy stops, still seething with anger. She needs an explanation; she waits for it. Her mother catches up to her and then strides toward the truck.

"I'm annoyed with you," she says, expressing her infuriation. She unlatches the truck door, sits, and slams it hard. Leona drives the truck. She's supposed to tell her.

"They were business partners."

"You knew him," Leona says as she looks at her daughter, exhales, and then focuses on the road.

"Once."

"And you think I would believe that?"

She gasps and throws an intent look, revealing a sense of regretful pride. Leona can't hide it anymore or keep it concealed from her daughter.

"Alright, maybe ten to twelve times."

Daisy keeps mum; she is not convinced, though she now believes they encountered each other quite a number of times.

Her sight catches the steady lighthouse in the distance. The coastline resonates with swells, the cries of gulls echo across its expanse. She can hear them distinctly. They are closer to their home. She makes up her mind; she will not go home until sunset. Leona stops the truck. A gulf of silence arises between them. Daisy gets out of the truck, but this time she's soft and easy.

"I will see you at sunset."

Leona nods, pulls over the truck, and leaves the space toward home. Daisy gazes at the ocean water, sets her foot, and marches ahead. The breeze talks through her skin, cold and shivering in her spine. The moisture extends its arms from the deep ocean to the coastline; the swells reverberate a hundred times, lapping the edges. She's silent and steady. Her feet feel the coarse dunes, the rough pebbles underneath, as she searches for the lightkeeper. She inspects, finds none, and concludes in the absence of any familiar faces. Daisy dawdles around and comes across a door at the base of the lighthouse. The basement has a huge empty chamber. It feels like a dungeon, dark and damp. Her footfalls echo through a series of steps. Then her searching fingers find the switch. The attic lights up. A cot, a table, and a chair are her first notices. On the other side, away from the cot, she finds boxes of tools, a shovel, a hammer, and ropes nailed to the stone wall. Most of the attic is empty and cold. She assumes the lighthouse keeper dwells here. On the table, she finds a notebook, a pen, and a torch. Adjacent to it, spare lamps are arranged on the floor in case of emergencies. There are some reflectors, stepped lenses, Fresnel lenses to fix, likely for the lamp at the top, she thinks. This is the first time she has seen the attic. Her father didn't use it for living but used it as a repository of materials. He used to return home by midnight and leave again at early dawn.

Daisy hears the humming of voices outside. She rushes out. It's the housekeeper. She takes him by surprise; his humming pauses. A rhyme that he learned in school.

"What are you doing here?"

"I am just waiting for you."

He loosens himself and fixes the rope along the line that nobody is supposed to cross.

"You're inspecting me about my job, right?"

She smiles, then drops down.

"Do you know any bars around here?"

"I could show you," says the lighthouse keeper.

Daisy doesn't return home that night. Her mother waits and comes up looking for her at the lighthouse. She finds no one. She's frightened, terrorized by thoughts that never let her fall asleep.

CHAPTER SIX

The Weekend Home

Susan calls her mother in the early hours of Friday morning. She maintains her gaze on the gleaming sun, burning out along the edges of the skyscraper on the east side of her apartment. Sipping her tea, she lingers back and forth on her balcony. Her physique outlines are distinctively proportioned, fit, radiative, and attractive in her racerback sports bra and appealing in her hipster undies. She has completed her morning workouts; a fitness enthusiast, she appears to be. The night, however, melted into provocative thoughts, keeping her awake long after. It was about a man at the bar, Alan, and the involvement of a woman in her late thirties, which she finds prejudiced. It makes her feel detached from all attempt. She contemplates the need to break the news to Tony.

"Alright, just for a week," she listens to her mother on the other side. "Please don't burden yourself unnecessarily."

"I read about your case two days ago."

She sips her tea. "Not now. Mother. I'll see you tomorrow. Just be prepared," she hangs up abruptly.

An hour later, she takes the elevator to the thirteenth floor. She's draped in her usual uniform and walks the aisles of cubicles, paying no heed to the rest. She strolls into her cabin without a methodical approach to greet others, her expressions latent. Unsettled, she muddles over the blatant clue from the man at the bar. She assesses it repeatedly until a convincing conclusion forms.

"What if Alan is correct?"

She doesn't want to miss this chance. A rigid conviction fastens in her fleeting mind. She absorbs details about the late-thirties woman, a hint or suggestion that might jeopardise her investigation. As for the eighteen-year-old girl, there are no details yet. She moves back and forth, her chair rolling in a zigzag. She can't decide whether to dismiss the matter or emphasize it. She's skeptical. Tony will be summoning her presence soon, while she sifts the entire plight, waiting for his call.

A knock arrives at her door. It's her subordinate, who enters and settles in a chair.

"He's asking for you," the subordinate says.

Susan nods, then retrieves a file from the drawer and hands it to her subordinate.

"I knew it. There are no details about the eighteen-year-old girl. There's something new I've learned," Susan mentions.

"What is it?"

"Hold on. I must see him first," says Susan.

She quickly leaves, rushing out of the door. The subordinate follows out in wonder. She doesn't follow her to Tony's chamber. Susan recklessly barges in without knocking.

"There's something I need to tell you," says Susan.

She feels the intensity within herself. It sounds urgent, demanding attention.

"Susan, I was expecting you," Tony responds.

She is not surprised by that, nor does she receive any comment following it; instead, she reacts in a serious manner, setting a tone for herself.

"There's another woman in her late thirties," Susan asserts.

Tony gazes at her skeptically. He's not convinced and is unwilling to believe her at first attempt. His gesture of refusal is clear.

"What's the source?" he questions.

"Alan. A guy I met at the bar last evening," says Susan, her tone persuasive.

She speaks with weight in her voice this time, her tone optimistic.

Tony locks his fingers, resting them on his elbow with his chin braced by the locked fingers. He thinks intuitively, getting a hunch of the situation.

"Well, bring him forth," he says.

"Sure, I do remember his face."

"What about the girl?"

"We are not there yet."

Tony clicks the mouse, reviewing the footage once again for himself on his desktop. "Get all the latest details – schools, social accounts, bank details, parents, friends – leave nothing to chance. Circulate her picture around the city."

Susan feels the need to inform him about her weekend trip to Chicago while promising to discern the details about the girl and fetching Alan to examine further possibilities regarding the murder of Blanford Sky upon her return.

"Give my regards to your mother," says Tony.

She makes a gentle gesture, followed by a glint of a smile as she exits the chamber. The clock ticks eleven a.m., the sunlight beams through her window shield. Automobiles honk on the road; she watches from the thirteenth floor. The city crowd resonates in numbers while she struggles to decipher what the eighteen-year-old girl's trouble might be in the days ahead. She makes an effort to recall the name of the Hotel...Hotel Grande Albergo delle Palme.

The subordinate appears again. Joe Cole is intrigued by what has happened inside. She barges into the chamber; her footfalls draw Susan's attention. She brings no new discovery, instead, a sort of curiousness revealing an outcast expression on her face.

"What happened inside?"

"Well, it appears a woman is involved too."

Joe gets the chair; she's clumsy and casual. Although she tries to insert herself in the scenario, her eyes blink unwittingly, falling short of her skills, of how she was never regarded as a part of this investigation. She feels envious about it but hesitates to admit the truth.

"Hope you're having a good time then."

Susan grins. "I need you to do me a favor. Could you take charge in my place in case I don't make it by Monday?"

"Where are you going?"

"Chicago. I need to get my mom."

"Okay, I'll do it," says Joe.

In a minute, she slips out of Susan's chamber. A development in their relationship makes her feel delighted, not that she didn't get to play a role in the investigation. Joe Cole has been in the New York Police for the last five years, straight after her graduation from the Academy. Since then, she has been posted in this city and never regretted it. Although in those five years she has been only a part of two investigations, she did well in both and expected more to come. But for her, this was a surprise, jolting in many ways due to her exclusion.

While Tony, being reckless and keen to find out about Alan, suggested measures to his subordinate to gather details about the man, it was noticed in the process that Alan had a record of robbery. He had spent six months in prison and was granted bail under conditions favorable to the police department. He had to help them solve cases of theft and report his whereabouts monthly, until the department felt confident about his situation.

A dropout of college, Alan finally learned to deal with robbery crimes, mastering the art with the input from the police and striving hard to lead a decent and sober life. Knowing he was still under watch, he couldn't escape until his debts were repaid as promised.

The astounding private affair that surfaced while scrutinizing Alan in regards to his operations was the brief job he had as an assistant to Blanford Sky. That raised series of doubts and miscalculations about his character. Tony seemed amazed; at the same time he had sense of fear about the man.

Tony forwarded the inputs to Susan about the man she was about to involve.

At five p.m., Susan shows up at the bar. She takes a counter chair. Her eyes survey around and finds Massy a couple of tables away. She watches her deliver the drinks, but she can't find the man she came looking for. She surrenders her effort and waits for her friend. Massy's hand falls on the counter table. She prepares a glass for her visiting friend.

"The regular?"

"No, give me something new," says Susan, fretting.

"Is something troubling you?"

"Where can I find Alan?"

Massy gives her a glass of espresso martini, unsure if that's what's bothering her.

"You're sounding like a cop now."

"Yes, I do because I am a cop. That's my job."

Massy doesn't get on with her. She apprehends the situation. It is not what she had been expecting this evening from her friend. However, she keeps it plain and sober.

"I don't have his address, but he visits every Friday. Give me a day."

"That won't be necessary; I'll see him on Friday."

Susan finishes her glass of espresso martini and waits for the faint light to die. She wants to be back when the darkness falls and the streets illuminate with lights around. She drifts back and forth, then sideways, fixing her gaze again on Massy.

"I think you need to go home."

She nods. "I'm sorry about my rude behavior; that was not my intention. You know it's the case."

"I understand."

"Thank you for tolerating."

Massy smiles. "You're my friend, and I know you're doing good."

Susan gets off her chair, preparing to leave. She sets her foot on the floor and walks out with simplified smile.

"See you tomorrow."

She stops at the door. "Sorry, I won't be available tomorrow. I'm going to get my mom from Chicago."

She waves at Massy and vanishes from her sight. She gets in the car, speeds between the lanes, and disappears among the crowd.

At ten a.m. in the morning, she texts her mother. Susan hurries to the airport. She reminds Joe Cole about Monday in case she fails to make it. Susan checks in through the gate, not hustling up in the security check line. Her ID works well, the

NYPD badge serving her for many purposes, granting easy access to forbidden zones. She takes the non-stop flight, a duration of two hours in the air. In the two hours, she tries to perceive the face of the woman involved in her head. She can feel and sense how she will look, replacing herself from her late twenties to late thirties. She outlines her body, her shape, how a woman in late thirties would look. She maneuvres her head skilfully, just in case she can figure out and find a woman in the late thirties on the plane. She shudders as the wheels land and she feels the crust of the Earth's surface. Susan smells the air as she gets off the plane. She feels at home, delighted about the change she appreciates for a short while. Her mother waits. She gets her car, a Ford Sedan in use for six years and more.

They hug each other and feel the distance close between them.

"Let me drive?"

"I have renewed my license," says her mother.

"I'm a cop; you know the deal."

Her mother grins and lets her. "That's the cop talking."

Susan chuckles, shifts the gear, and takes the road home.

CHAPTER SEVEN

In The Lighthouse

At the stroke of early dawn, a knock echoes at the door – a silent, calm sound. The commotion resonates around; even the rooster doesn't crow. It's still too early for the break of dawn. Daisy Collins taps again. It feels terrible. She can feel the stir of breeze from the coast. She waits for her mother to open the door. Leona hears it this time. She gets out of bed, shuffles her feet, and speaks in her light tone.

"Who is it?"

No response. Then a sense of legitimate fear creeps within her. She moves slowly toward the door, getting close enough to discern the figure on the opposite side. Her mental picture shapes about her missing daughter. She hopes it's not the light keeper, she prays. Omens stir up in her head about Daisy. She's possessive and scared at the same time, clinging onto her daughter's safety above all. Leona Hill opens the door and sees Daisy looking worse for wear. Her clothes half-drawn, portions of her body exposed. She has not returned the same. She's wearing a man's shirt; her jeans are missing below. The shirt covers her thighs, oversized and disorderly. Her hair is messy. The shirt smells of men's perfume. She appears chaotic.

"Where have you been?"

Leona's voice sounds panicked, tender, caring, and at the same time, fearful. She's suspects some untold, terrible activity involving her daughter. Daisy smells of alcohol. She looks dreadful overall. Instead of responding to her mother, she lumbers upstairs to her room.

"Are you alright, sweetheart?"

Leona sighs; she's certain something has gone wrong. She waits at the kitchen table while frying a slice of bacon. Through the window, she can see the front yard and the far-stretching coastline. The lighthouse is a little distance away. She calls for her daughter but sees no sign of her. She waits and watches the dawn break. The faint light glimmers at the edge of horizon. She grows worried and panicked.

The tap water fills the tub, creaking as Daisy turns it off. She adds cold water. Still wearing the shirt, she steps into the tub. As the water moderates, she loosens her buttons and lets the shirt gently drop to the floor. It still smells of alcohol, a strong spirit she had never tried before. She feels dizzy and inefficient. She raises her right leg and plunges it into the water, followed by the left. In seconds she is immersed in the water, feeling warm and cozy. Her body drifts, floating. The entire tub fits her. She inhales deeply and ducks her head under the water, remaining there. She can replay what happened at the lighthouse. It makes her relive the events.

When the road appears dark and silent, even the loudest noise fails to draw attention. The truck reaches the lighthouse and the bar shuts down. Daisy is the last person to leave for the night. Drunk, she doesn't talk or grumble, only fussing about her mother. She falls half asleep. Her eyes partly open, she is only half-conscious of her surroundings. The truck stops and she shudders. She feels the hands against her, trying to lift her. She can feel her weight being transported. She hears the footfalls of a boot, and the metal door creaks. Her hazy vision obscures her view, but the surroundings seem familiar. The series of steps reminds her of a hollow attic, resembling a dungeon. She can't do anything about it; she's drunk, weak, and delicate. Suddenly, she feels the comfort of a bed. Through bleary eyes, she recognizes the attic's vault. She feels warm; the overdose of alcohol makes her sense that. She babbles, asking for attention. Her tank top exposes her upper body, outlines her breast distinctly, bulging and soft. Her lower body is covered in jeans. The lighthouse keeper watches her, a wicked play rolling in the minds of the devil. He can't remain silent. The hormones rush, urging him to make a move. He finds it spine-chilling, but his urges compel him.

The fine intention turns wild. The man falls on top of her. He attempts to kiss Daisy. For a few seconds, she tries to circumvent, but her effort fails. She senses the touch of his lips on her, crawling down her belly. She surrenders. The man pulls off her clothes. The lighthouse keeper fucks her. And fucks well. Daisy remembers it all.

The door batters with hard blows. It's her mother. She sounds frustrated and baffled.

"I need to talk to you."

Daisy doesn't hear. The knock continues, each strike harder than the last. Leona's fright increases. She can't keep it off. She waits, but the battering continues. In the tub, Daisy feels the vibration. The water seems to talk to her, echoing in her ear. Suddenly, she senses a jolt. It shivers her spine, and she ducks her head out of the water.

"I'm washing myself," she screams.

"I need you down immediately."

She hears her mother's footfalls descending. Daisy intends to stay a little longer, washing herself with warm water. Certainly, she's not perturbed by what she has done. She stands in front of her mirror after finishing her bath. Nude and well fit, she sees her figure outlined in the reflection. She watches the break of the day from her window, hearing the calming sound of waves hitting the shore. She examines herself from top to bottom, ensuring there are no marks on her. She feels good about herself and the sex she had. Her hand caress her private parts; she touches and feels safe about it. She can say now she's no longer a virgin – an eighteen-year-old adult. However, it reminds her that she can never fall in love with the lighthouse keeper. It has to do with her stiff emotions, which she can't divulge with the rest. She's a murderer, she knows well. But on this occasion, there was no covenant to kill the lighthouse keeper; she had allowed herself to be used. In her eyes, the house keeper stands innocent.

Daisy makes a swift move, feeling her hesitation through the stairs. She frames her thoughts, preparing what she's supposed to tell her mother. In other words, she must convince her by all means. This part of her life feels too personal to discuss. She's eighteen now, with the right to make decisions about her life. It shouldn't trouble anyone else. She hadn't felt this vexatious or formidable even when she was escaping from hotel Grande Albergo delle Palme. Her footfalls reach the ground floor. Leona turns her heavy head toward her, gazing intently.

"How are you feeling now?"

"Good."

"I made you a bacon slice."

Daisy takes the chair adjacent to her mother and glances at her. She can read her face, a whole grave of intents and doubts, uncertainty surfacing. She doesn't talk; instead, she cuts the bacon slice and puts it in her mouth.

"Aren't you gonna tell me what went wrong?" Leona presses her voice.

A glitch of exasperation bursts out. Daisy feels compulsive about it. She knows it isn't supposed to be talked about. She attempts to put away the discussion through a simple gesture.

"Nothing went wrong, Mother."

"You were half-naked this dawn, and you say nothing went wrong?"

The voice echoes, inflames, and dictates the current demand. No reply. Leona can't sustain her anger. She feels terrible in a horrifying way. She leaves the kitchen in the front yard, feeling inefficient and inadequate for all that she has been expecting. Mad at all things. Enraged by her daughter's demeanour.

"You have no right to talk to me that way," Daisy advances.

The voice rides Leona's nerves. She felt the pulse running, the angst it carried. It's the toxic sentiment that needed its expression.

"For god's sake, I'm your mother."

Daisy's eyes sprinkle in the morning light. Her gestures appear irresponsible, an act she isn't aware of. Her feet drag closer, cold and heavy. She doesn't mind the intensity, the fierce face of her mother. She can't keep hurting her, she realizes. She has seen in the past. And now she stands as a criminal before her. The truth is that each of them played a part in the murder of Blanford Sky. Daisy exhales, ready to break the gulf of silence.

"I just got drunk. We made out."

Leona stands stiff and turns her face. She isn't scared to look in the eyes. She tries to be intimidating but fails to administer it. Her daughter isn't the same anymore.

"Do you love him?"

The complex perplexity exhibits no real intention. Daisy turns her eyes away from her mother. Then, it faces toward the coast. She, in turn, cannot hum the truth of the feeling. She assures herself again she isn't in love with the lighthouse keeper. Eventually, she utters the same thing as she decides spontaneously.

"No."

She keeps it short.

Leona breathes in. A certain trait of relaxation she exhibits. However, she can't believe that an imprudent act took place. A disgrace of feeling she stands with.

"You disappointed me."

She sidles inside the house.

At sunset, the music buzzes aloud. The truck door opens, and the vibration resonates in the surroundings. The rock music scares the homecoming birds. The gulls divert their way on a different path. The swells lap a thousand times along the coast. In the dock, the chainsaw whines, tearing wood into pieces. The lighthouse keeper is equipped with a hammer, nails, and wood plank next to him. The wreck dock is being made. At the top of the lighthouse, the lamp gets concentrated, its glow visible from the distance on the vast ocean ahead. He laughs aloud, flashing a wicked smile; it's the night that he imagines in his head – sex with the girl. He can't stay away rolling it over and over, only to find out sooner about Daisy's visit. He gazes in the direction, the stone walls in the view, the house in his vision, and the vantage point allows him to draw closer. He laughs again, then smiles wickedly. It surfaces distinctly, his mischievous purpose. The desire doubles for Daisy Collins in his lucid dream.

CHAPTER EIGHT

The Accused

The crowd, the tall buildings, and the skyscrapers fascinate her. She stretches her gaze from the balcony. In the distance, the beam arrives, tingles on her furrowed skin, and she feels elated at the morning hour. The old woman finds herself surrounded by chaos. A hoarding displays the face of a girl with essential information. The accused in the picture is an eighteen-year-old girl. A bounty of 5,000 US dollars goes to those who could help locate her. Blanford Sky is seen next to her. The accused is being pressed for the murder of the Statesman. The old woman reads the rudimentary details from her balcony. Her vision is too poor to catch those words. She struggles. She reads The Suspect.

Name: Daisy Collins
Age: 18 years
Address: Yet Unknown
Nationality: American
Skin Color: White
Height: Yet Unknown
Occupation: School Girl
Accused: Murder of Statesman, Blanford Sky
Bounty: $5000

Status: Unidentified. Report to the New York State Police Department for the bounty.

The footfall follows her. It's her daughter, Susan Kelly. She gets a cup of tea for her mother. Then, she joins her before she leaves on the errand to catch the eighteen-year-old girl. Susan keeps the cup on the edge of the balcony parapet. She rests her arms, adding to the gazing. The city's sunlight smears across the sky.

"You should drink the tea before it gets cold."

"What a poor girl."

Susan turns her face away from the hoarding. She prepares her mind for what she's supposed to tell Tony. She watches the clock tick eight.

"You shouldn't be pitiful about her. She committed a crime," said Susan.

She walks in, dressing herself in the uniform. She's supposed to be on the thirteenth floor by nine, or else her accountability gets questioned.

"She's so young and beautiful. How preposterous!"

Susan hears her mother's old talk. She passes over, allowing her to ponder her ancient, poignant heart. Susan's prime motive is clear for the week. It's the man at the bar this Friday, she remembers sharply, as said by her friend. Alan will face her again, and this time he will have to answer. Susan has been waiting impatiently over the weekend. This encounter might get her close to the suspect. At nine, she reaches her workplace on the thirteenth floor. She gets summoned by Tony. Monday morning gets robust, anticipating many unknown conquests. Unclear and uncertain about where she's headed with none to answer her. Nor does she get any sort of detail about the girl. But, the woman in her late thirties cages her above all. She needs the truth. Her mother is supposed to leave by Sunday; a week's stay seems to be enough to tolerate the urban chaos of New York.

On Friday evening, Susan shows up at the bar. She occupies the counter, tired and exhausted; her pretty eyes shimmer with loneliness. She drops her head on the table and waits for a voice to be heard.

"You look terrible."

She lifts her head, sifts the corner around, and then looks up at Massy's face.

"Get me a plain martini."

She doesn't find Alan, and she doesn't even have an impression.

"What's with the eighteen-year-old accused, Daisy Collins?"

Massy sets the glass down. She leans forward, her hands comfortably resting on the counter table. She waits to hear from the cop.

"It's hard to tell yet," says Susan.

"$5000, seriously."

"NYPD is rich," Susan titters.

She takes another sip and scans the room. She finds no one familiar.

"Are you sure he will show up?"

"Usually he does," Massy says. "Why don't you take another glass while you wait?"

The sun goes down and the street lights brighten. The Broadway appears crowded, and the taxis line up waiting for the green signal. Yes, the yellow paint New York Taxis. The swarm of people never completes from both the end. Susan waits, drinks another plain martini, and shares her mother's opinion with her friend about the city. Then, a creak of the door seizes her attention. It's Alan walking in, aiming for the counter.

"It's him, Alan," says Massy.

He takes the chair as usual. He smiles at Massy and gets the drink he prefers. Massy is kind enough to serve him well. She can't lose him, the daily Friday Man. In time, he has become a regular face in the bar.

"How are you doing, Alan?"

Massy gets him the drink.

"Good."

He keeps it short. He isn't aware of the presence of the cop. Susan monitors him from the corner. Though she can't find anything suspicious about the man, her prime intent lingers. She's here to find out about the woman he mentioned. Alan takes a sip and relaxes. He's been jobless ever since he worked as an assistant to Blanford Sky.

"Hello, Alan."

The voice ruptures him. He lifts his head to look at the strange voice. He finds the face familiar. Then he pulls his eyes away from her. Something is queer here, he senses.

"What do you want from me?"

Susan takes a seat next to him. She watches him light a cigarette. The gust of smoke airs out of his mouth.

"I need you to tell me about the woman."

He plays with his cigarette, twitching his fingers. Alan turns his face toward her. Not a smooth expression, though. He finishes his drink and gets really heavy.

"What do you want to know? Do you want to know about the woman who killed Blanford Sky?"

Susan looks at him with a watchful eye, keen enough to deduce the bitterness he owns. She keeps silent for seconds.

"Do you have a job?"

"Why do you care?"

Susan peers as his cigarette shortens. "I can help you get one," she pauses. "You could work with me."

He titters. "You're asking me to help you?"

"Yes. You will be paid for this. We could make a great team. You could restart your life. This is an opportunity, you don't want to miss it."

Alan squashes his cigarette in the ashtray and involves himself in prolonged thought of consideration, though his silence suggests otherwise. He glances at Susan, who is hard to trust but fair in the play. He needs money, and he knows that well. He nods his head, assertive, yearning for the job.

"Here's my card. Report to me tomorrow at nine," says Susan.

He reads it well. The New York State Police Department logo. The headquarters' address and the department are on the thirteenth floor. Susan leaves the bar after one last exchange of words with her friend. She expresses her gratitude toward Massy for the drink and for helping her find the man. She waves at her at the exit door. Massy pulls her gaze away from her friend, then reverts to Alan.

"Do you need another glass?"

"It was you."

A despicable expression surges on Alan's face. He isn't happy about it, nor can he complain.

"I couldn't help. She's a cop."

Massy gets him a drink. She watches him quaffing at once.

"It's not your fault. I knew she would come looking for me since I first met her."

He stands on his feet. Then, he looks at his watch. It's time for him to go home. He burns a cigarette while his feet limp around. He gets the awkward walk following the exit door.

"I'll see you on Friday," says Alan.

The clock ticks eleven; Massy waits for the last man to exit the door. She's exhausted and sleepy at the same time. The outside street helps her stay awake until she shuts the bar. By the time she leaves home, she's alone, walking on the street. And with every lamp post she passes, she can see the face of an eighteen-year-old girl, Daisy Collins. It's in every corner of the city. The chaos becomes vital when a group of men passes her, talking about the bounty. She's afraid now to take a step ahead when she reads the bulletin on one lamp post. She gestures for a taxi. She's fortunate to have hired one. She breathes in and tries hard to keep herself calm and still. She imagines all she can about Daisy Collins. Within her, she expresses pity and sympathizes with the situation. The chase and the hunt have already begun.

CHAPTER NINE

The Chase

Three weeks after the bounty bill announcement, the report surfaces on the television. It's on every news channel. The chase escalates. Daisy Collins is everywhere. She's a criminalized celebrity. The entire nation knows about the girl. The New York Times's headline read, **Justice is being Chased,** in bold typeface. Aside from the paragraph, a caricature portrays Daisy Collins plunging a knife into the chest of the erstwhile Statesman, Blanford Sky. It's a scary, serious joke; no one laughed. The caricature has received immense popularity in an infamous way. It has come to notice, at Broadway Theatre, a play has been performed. The caricature has turned into a sexual symbol, and in the play, it demonstrates a man trying to rape a girl. In an act of retaliation, the girl stabs a knife to save herself. A great imitation of the murdered Statesman. People rejoiced and laughed.

Susan Kelly reads at her table, knowing the matter has been dramatized. She blames the New York Times.

The clock ticks five o' clock, and Daisy's vision flickers in the descending beam. She watches the fading rays disappear from her window. For three weeks, she has not gone out. Since then, her relationship with Leona has grown healthier. She misses the beach and the lighthouse. Although her window gives her a vantage point, it also gives her an access to the coast. She hears the lapping of swells and the cry of gulls. At night, she watches the lamp light rotate across the ocean. She thinks and regrets her incautious action. She can't love the lighthouse keeper, now it troubles her for the sex. The twilight fades below the horizon, and she closes the book she has been reading. In the distance, it catches her attention – the buzz of a truck engine. It gets louder as it travels closer. She cranes herself through the window. It's the lighthouse keeper, she recognizes the truck. She keeps her attentive gaze fixed. Then the sound diverts in the opposite direction. The bar, she construes. Daisy breathes, then relaxes on her chair. She's supposed to help her mother in the kitchen. That morning, she was informed about a guest arriving. It's Leona's friend from the other town. Although she hates the kitchen stuff, she didn't want to ruin it anymore. She descends and gets absorbed in the kitchen with her mother. Daisy can't hide her hunch. She feels terrible about it. She breaks her silence.

"I saw him go to the bar."

Leona bids her silent character goodbye. Something happened that evening. That she's not willing to unfurl is a secret. She appears cryptic, a notion that was never seen before.

"Are you fine with him?"

Daisy speaks nothing; she glances at her mother once and returns to her work. She senses something is wrong with her. Her conduct isn't the same. For her, it seems nothing has happened and that she's entirely fine with it. Daisy discovers the television set isn't on the dining table.

"Where's the television set?"

"I packed it inside," says Leona.

"It wasn't necessary."

Leona peers at her and says, "We've got a guest tonight, and we've a very small space to dine on the table."

Daisy isn't convinced by those words. Somehow, she completes her stuff in the kitchen and waits for the guest's arrival.

An hour ago, the television was buzzing with news of the chase. To her dismay, Leona stood watching from her spot in the kitchen, feeling unsteady. She shambled over to lower the volume of the TV set. She didn't want it to be heard outside. Daisy appeared on the screen alongside the victim, Blanford Sky. Leona's spine shivered in fear, and she trembled in shock. She wanted to hide it all from her daughter. The bounty was high: $5,000. The tremor unsettled her deeply; *the police had found her,* a troubling realization she had feared might come true. She was running short of decisive measures. Her hands fumbled, and she swallowed the blob of saliva in her mouth. Her body perspired in panic. Leona didn't want to go to prison; she's afraid of it, but she's involved in the murder of the Statesman. She imagined herself as an inmate, which terrified her even more. She had to do something to get rid of this; her fearful mind whined at her. She immediately wrapped the television. She knew Daisy could be dangerous; she might inadvertently expose the plot of the Statesman's assassination. With her everywhere, the police would inevitably come knocking at their door. Leona couldn't let that happen, her intentions now turning desperate to protect herself. She was on a new path, this time involving her daughter. Of all the knowledge Daisy had, this detail failed her, leaving her oblivious and unaware.

At the bar, the keeper orders another glass of beer. The porch twinkles with a series of decorative lights. Trucks and cars are parked nearby. A few yards away, the ocean water laps at the edge, its roar distinct to the ears. Music plays softly in the background. He watches the bartender drop his glass of beer, then shifts his focus toward the television. The news startles the patrons, and the headlines sound terrific. Images of Daisy Collins and Blanford Sky distinctly appear on the screen. The bounty announced is a tempting amount that excites those chasing it. The keeper remains fixated on the screen, astounded and taken aback by what he sees. It sends shiver down his spines, prompting memories of the night he had. The night of sex he misses dearly, yet now he knows Daisy is a suspect. And the money he desires. He devours his glass of beer and lights a cigarette. He walks out of the bar onto the porch and puffs his cigarette rhythmically, then returns to his seat. His expression is bewildered, muddled by the reality sinking in.

The keeper clears his throat.

"Can I get another glass?"

He checks his watch and assures the time for himself. This night isn't empty, he reminds himself. The money comes into his wicked brain. Then he twitches back and forth in his seat. His intention was to examine if anyone present was paying attention to the television. Most did, baffling over the issue; some even projected a lie, like they know the girl or have seen her. It's the greed for the reward that talks. The keeper gets his share of beer and gulps instantly. He waits no longer, steering the truck along the way. He gets tipsy from an overdose of drink, then his vision begins to flicker in the beam of cars that pass by. Although his hands are stiff, the steering wheel is under control. Suddenly, he loses his sway at the speed, the brake fails, the truck tire skids in the runaway, and he crashes into the pole. In seconds, he finds his vision going dark and blinds out. A drop of blood smears on his head, showing the forehead is injured. A dent forms in the truck's hood. Over it, the pole splits into two, falling heavily. Unmovable and stuck, the truck stops. Smoke spouts from the hood, and the heated engine halts. The keeper falls unconscious, resting his head over the steering wheel. Hands fall free of his shoulder. No vehicle pass by unnoticed on the empty way; they rarely traveled at this hour. Most sightings are of those returning from the bar. On this particular evening, the bar remains open until late night. Thirty minutes later medical help arrives. The keeper is put into the ambulance and taken to the nearby town's hospital.

Leona greets her friend with a goodnight wish. The serene night speaks of none; a roar of the swells visits nearby. Daisy watches her mother in the front yard as the guest leaves. She searches for the presence of light from the distant lamp. It misses, even a tiny beam lacks focus. She steps inside and wades into her room. The solitude prevails around, the breeze culminates in a dense manner, a drizzle to come soon. Leona looks in the direction of the shore. It's dark, no sign of the beam. Something's wrong, her gut says. She trudges inside and shuts the door. The thud matches the tiddly, thundering cry of black clouds. It's about to rain. For long, the headlines bother her, and in addition, they keep her confounded about the keeper's absence at the lighthouse. Her intention remains rigid – the possibility of getting rid of her daughter. She doesn't want to end up in a prison with her, fearing the imminent knock on her door by the police. Moreover, she now depends on the keeper.

Upstairs, in the room, Daisy opens her window and grips the novel she intends to finish. The drizzle begins to pour on the rooftop. In the distance, her vantage point provides easy access toward the shore. The lappings are near; the ocean water blares in ripples. Her murky vision sights the stationed boat along the deck, the ropes holding it tight first, followed by the lighthouse. Then at the lighthouse that sparks in frequent lightning glows. Then she opens the page. The pitter-patter of the rainwater joins her in the words. She reads.

The next morning, the clear sky exhibits empty space. The warming beam falls on the deprived land, which brings joy to the creatures. The chirping birds release their nests, and the gulls cry in delight as they patrol over the sky to the ocean. Leona watches from the edge of her stone wall. She anticipates the presence of the lighthouse keeper. But the truck goes missing. Her aspiration gets vandalized. She continues to wait for the day. She gets inside. The footfalls thump the wooden stairs, and in a series of well-behaved chaos comes down Daisy. She's skeptical of what she has seen through her window in the last fifteen minutes. She finds her mother in the living room, arranging a series of vases with newly installed flowers in them.

"Are you hiding something from me?" Daisy asks.

Leona turns her head, feigning ignorance, to dispel any suspicion.

"What makes you think that?"

"Just curious. Things have been going off lately."

Daisy waits on the couch. She watches her mother's skills. When she's done, she sits next to her.

"I know what's troubling you," Leona gasps. "It's the argument about last night. Darling, you can have the television set in your room," she says.

"No, it's not about the television. You were seen waiting for the lighthouse keeper this morning."

"I have some business to do with him. It doesn't concern you."

She walks off to the kitchen. Daisy assembles her thoughts, pondering unmoved. She withdraws herself from her isolated ambience when she hears her mother call from the kitchen.

"You can help me if you're free."

Daisy reluctantly trudges into the kitchen and is assigned to do the dishes. She cranes her neck through the window, feeling the warm breeze slither in. Something vexes her, confronting within. Is it the police tracing me? Her mind talks. Or is it that her mother hiding something? Curiosity sets in, driven by the need to unravel the discomfort.

At noon, she slips into her room, eager to catch up on the updates about the investigation. She checks her phone. The New York Times pops up on the screen. She's a few days behind, scrolling over the headlines from the past weekend. "Justice being chased", she reads. The caricature paints a vivid picture. She feels tampered with and loses her mental grip. She sits on the chair and looks out through the window. A sign of distress and fear succumbs to her face. Deep within, her angst grows. Her anger multiplies on Leona. She feels betrayed. Leona is hatching a trap against her, Daisy learns that well. She takes a stand for herself. With a conviction she devises not to let Leona escape from the trick. Daisy decides not to be deceived by her again. She thinks she will act normally as if nothing came to her knowledge.

At sunset, Leona walks along the coastline. This time, she finds the basement door unlocked. The lighthouse is in operation. The beam stretches for miles toward the ocean. She ambles around, then knocks at the door. She hears none. It creaks as it opens. The hollow attic is lit. Leona walks down the series of steps. She breathes as her footfalls echo in the hollow space. Then her vision spots the injured lighthouse keeper. He's on bed rest. She walks closer, grabs a seat beside him and offers him comforting remedies.

In the window, Daisy traces her mother. She gets the grasp of it. Then she turns her sight toward the ocean. The beam focuses on the distance as the horizon turns from yellow to lightless darkness. She observes keenly, finding solace in returning to her unfinished book.

CHAPTER TEN

The New York State Police Department

Alan feels that the job would help him sustain himself. Having been out of work for months, he finally sets himself to work for the New York State Police Department as an undercover informant. He needs money; he knows that well. His options had run out, leaving him no choice but to assist the NYPD with the mystery case. He isn't assigned any rank, just classified as an agent for Susan.

Though he is familiar to her, on the day he is supposed to show up, hesitation grips him as he enters the building. On the thirteenth floor, he finds rows of desktops overpopulated with uniforms. "The so-called cops," he thinks to himself. His feet struggles as fear envelops his mind. He needs to find the right person; he passes through the aisle and helps himself to a conversation.

"Susan Kelly," he states.

A cop points him in the right direction. He sees two doors a few feet apart. He reads the tag labels, and one door creaks open, letting in a beam from the outside. Susan raises her head from a file.

"You're not a disappointing man," she says.

He takes a chair and feels fine for a while.

"It was hell getting here."

Susan smiles. "The boss has been waiting for you."

"What now? Am I a suspect?"

"It's just an introduction, a kind of protocol. There's nothing to panic about."

She gets up and walks out. He follows her.

Tony sorts the files on the table. The knock reaches him. He sets aside the papers and eyes them as they enter. He gestures for them to sit.

"Is he the one?" Susan nods. Alan feels scrutinized; he stands as a suspect. He proceeds closer and grabs a chair. He receives the intense vibes rolling onto him. He breaths, glancing back and forth. He waits for Tony's words.

"Do you know the consequences of deceiving?" Tony asks.

"Am I a suspect?"

Tony breathes, projecting calm.

"No, but you're under the radar," he says.

"I assumed that."

Tony focuses on Susan. He is not likely impressed by the progress.

"You know what you're supposed to do now."

"He's a useful man, a skilled fellow," she adds.

"Are you aware of what we are dealing with?"

Tony looks at Alan.

"If I'm not wrong, it's a caricature drama."

"That was stupid of the press."

Alan titters. "It made a whole lot of money at Broadway."

"How was it working with Blanford Sky?" Susan interjects.

Alan's expression turns crafty.

"Quite a tricky guy," he adds.

"How did you get the job of an assistant?" Tony lights a cigar and waits for his answer. He seems quite fine with Alan's silence. It doesn't matter much in their investigation. Alan hesitates, folding his arms.

"He needed an assistant, and fortunately I was just there at the right time."

Tony exhales, stands up, and pats Alan on the back.

"Welcome aboard," he says.

"Is he always like that?" Alan asks Susan.

Susan gasps. "I have never seen him that way. He's counting on you."

Alan follows Susan's footsteps into the office. He finds the officers cocky and unwelcoming. It is quite a sophisticated place to work with people in badges and blistering temperaments.

"Tell me about the woman," Susan asks.

The chair moves, the files are placed aside, and the monitor faces her. She flickers her eyes in the setting beam, moving away from the window. Alan rests himself in his chair. The struggle can be seen. He somehow frames the face of the woman in the late thirties.

"I once heard Blanford call her Leona."

The name draws her attention. "Leona," Susan repeats.

Alan stands abruptly. "I think I have done enough for today."

Susan sighs and checks the clock on the right. She invites him for a drink at the bar.

"Why not come to the bar with me?"

Alan gapes at her, not sure why she was proposing the idea. "Today's not Friday."

"Oh! I see. You're a Friday visitor. See you tomorrow, then."

He nods awkwardly.

Meanwhile, Susan searches the database; the name Leona appears frequently, but she doesn't know her last name. The suspect list is long, making it tedious to find the right person with limited information. She keeps the list intact and processes it on her server for detection. However, she requires the assistance of Alan to be more precise than just about the name. She ends her day and prepares to go home. But first, she decides to visit her friend at the bar.

When the sun goes down, the streets glitter, and Susan finds herself at the bar. Massy serves her the usual drink and leans her hand on the counter.

"So, how was Alan?" Massy asks.

"Excessively casual. He needs moulding."

"Does he really know anything about the woman?"

"Leona, that's what he said."

"And you highly doubt that?"

Susan finishes her drink. "I can't say that until I find out myself."

The clock strikes nine, and Manhattan's streets flood with diverse crowds. She watches them as they walk by her, back and forth in all directions.

"What now?" Massy asks.

"Nothing. My mother is in town. I have to drop her off at the airport this Sunday."

"Why didn't you tell me? I would love to meet her."

"Why don't you come for dinner tonight?"

"Great! That would be nice."

Massy closes her bar at ten and follows Susan to her home, where they share dinner with Susan's mother. By midnight,

Massy becomes quite familiar with the old woman. She finds her charming and sensible. Susan drops Massy off at home. They had spent a recreational evening. It makes her feel authentic. Susan stops the car.

"It was nice of you to come."

"Your mother is a wonderful woman."

Susan grins. "She isn't the same always."

"Good night."

Massy watches her drive past. The tail lights vanish from her sight. She returns home.

On Sunday, Susan drops her mother off at the airport.

CHAPTER ELEVEN

Below the Attic

The lighthouse keeper wakes up, skeptical of what he heard the other night. An uninvited guest, in his familiar form, appears in his dwelling. For a long time, his impression of Leona deserved gentle respect. But after the night, it changed quite a lot. He tries to recall the accident he had and the caricature he saw on television. The bar reminds him of all that. For now, he doesn't know where to set his foot. The cold floor sends shivers down his spine and tumbles before he straightens himself. His head hurts, the wound wrapped over and over, reminding him of Leona's daunting intention. His vision settles in the hollow attic as he struggles to walk up the series of steps to be outside. The door creaks, opens, and he feels the first beam blinding his vision for seconds. He walks out in the open, lamely. He finds his working tool spread out and unsettled in the area. He gathers them one by one. The coast roars, but it is composed of sunny days with no alteration of harsh wind. It's breezy, though. He remarks about the good weather. Then he takes a walk toward the dock.

His gaze is directed at the stone wall, yards away from him. It's clear and sharp. The focus is hard, and his mind creeps over and over. He cannot refuse to disobey or reject what is being told to him. Leona now depends on him for the next offense. It has to deal with someone's life. He thinks it's brutal to betray someone he has slept with. His long anticipation may not respond well; the reason is unclear.

Why would Daisy murder the Statesman?

The question confounds him. It must have been a trap she was set into. Her mother. However, the lighthouse keeper didn't have any knowledge about the Statesman's relevance. He watches the horizon lit in color, and then the rising sun emerges in bright shades. He cares of none while he ponders over his mind. He feels the tool box in his hand and decides not to work that day. It's the night's accident. He hears the echo of the ocean, then relaxes into a mild notion.

In the glow of the morning beam, Daisy strolls along the sandy coast. She feels the tiny gravels prodding at her feet. She covers herself with a shawl as she nears the shore. The breeze traces her. The lighthouse keeper watches her appear as she closes in. Daisy lands softly at the dock. She isn't afraid, nor does she avoid eye contact. She inhales deeply, then clears her throat. Her arms folded, she cups herself.

"How are you doing?"

"Good."

Something has changed in the attitude of the keeper. He seems sober and gentle. A kind gesture is a very rare trait to contemplate.

"I heard about the accident."

The lighthouse keeper nods his head, then faces toward the ocean. He's skeptical of what he's supposed to say, for his intention seems quite assertive in his behavior.

"I'm fine with it."

Daisy looks at him fondly. She's in search of deeper understanding of what she has seen in the last few hours. She knows the plot, the conspiracy being cast upon her. However, she needs to hear from the keeper. She talks about her mother's visit.

"My mother is framing me. She's using you."

This startles the lighthouse keeper. He stands in wreck. A well-defined expression outlines his face – perplexed, confounded, uncertainty that ensemble him inappropriately. He struggles to face her.

"She revealed to me about the Statesman."

"Yes, it was me."

The keeper acutely glares at her face. He's short of words, and that begins to trouble him. His question resurfaces, an exploration of the story is what he urges for. He waits for Daisy to recount the tragic episode. His question begins as simple inquiry.

"Why did your mother want to kill the Statesman?"

She inhales deeply, then relaxes, leaning on the edge of the deck. She slumps closer to the keeper, both keeping their eyes open, gazing at the distant horizon.

"She had an affair."

The lighthouse keeper glances at her, then looks back toward the ocean water. He isn't sure what he's supposed to say.

"Your mother came with an intention. You must stay safe."

Daisy senses it, feeling the breeze rush through her. The beam overhead directs upwards. In the distance, the chaos of gulls hovers across the clear sky. Returning to the coast, the silky glow of sand attracts the birds. She silences her chit-chat. Seconds pass, turning into minutes. Closest to her understanding, she breaks after her extended pause.

"She wants to get rid of me."

She shows no hint of emotions nor fear creeping upon her.

"And how did she choose to do that?" she adds, questioning.

Timidity flashes across the lighthouse keeper's countenance. Unsure of what he's supposed to answer, his silence is broadly understood. His dry lips gesture an unwanted song, fiddling with the notion of fear unfurling onto him. He keeps his words tucked underneath and reaches for his toolbox.

"You should go now. Your mother wouldn't find this good," he says.

Daisy waits, facing toward the ocean water. She says nothing; instead, her vision shares the ocean's color. The breeze multiplies, the winnow resonates. In the distance, the cargo ship blows its whistle.

"It doesn't bother me anymore."

"Why don't you come into the attic?"

"Pretending to be sober."

The keeper grins at her. "I can't help myself."

She follows him. Her steps tenderly falls on the age-old staircase. The footfalls grow faint as she touches the cold floor. Then the light brightens. She wanders around the stone-carved wall, then checks around.

"You haven't changed anything."

"Just the way I like."

The keeper sets the toolbox under the table. His gaze fixes on her standing close by the bed. He inches closer to her, pulling a chilled ice box from underneath.

"What's inside the box?"

"Do you want some beer?"

An insisting, compelling voice resonates inside the attic. Daisy sits along the edge of the bed.

"Sure," she nods.

Her hand reaches for the beer. It's chilled, and she can feel the wetness dripping through her fingers. The keeper takes a chair, engaging in their conversation. His intentions seem sober and gentle, much in favor of her. However, he's clueless about what lies ahead for him. He takes note of what he's unaware of.

"What went wrong with the affair?"

Momentarily, Daisy feels a surge of nervous tension. She sips her bottle of beer, trying her best to stay steady. She keeps her words silent, grasping for air. She hesitates to recount the tale, ending it abruptly.

"An argument."

She strolls around, then heads up the stairs. Her gestures simplify as she follows her instincts. The sun overhead beams down as she wanders out into the open. The keeper follows her out of the attic, watching her closely.

"I should get going," says Daisy.

"I'll see you around then."

She nods and walks off. Her feet traverse the loosely packed gravel, feeling the warmth of sand climb between her toes.

"Thank you for rebuilding the dock."

Her voice rises in gratitude. The keeper gently nods. His stare remains fixed on her until she diminishes in the distance.

The clock strikes nine p.m., and silence falls. Daisy puts away her book and refocuses. She hears the shrill tone of her mother's voice. The gist is harrowing. Her feet touch the cold floor, moving steadily toward the window. The breeze brushes through as the window flap remains open. She catches sight of the lighthouse tower, its beam sharpening into the distance, keeping a long surveillance. She shuts the window, mentally preparing for the upcoming confrontation. Her mother calls again, closer this time, steps away on the stair deck. Daisy hurries down without a second thought. It's dinner time. The table is set, plates empty. Leona urges her daughter, politely, to sit next to her. But there's a silence, a commotion running from head to toe that only Daisy feels. She distinctly hears the sound of water being poured into her glass. Though she feels the need to be grateful to her mother, she remains quiet. She sips from her glass, then begins with the bread.

"You shouldn't visit the man at the coast."

"I find nothing wrong with him," says Daisy.

Leona expresses a sense of discomfort. Her face turns morose.

"You know what he did to you."

"He did nothing wrong. We just hooked up one night, that's all."

"You do not know the threat a man can bring."

Daisy breathes out, facile and simplistic in her portrayal.

"But you do know how a woman can destroy a man."

Leona gropes for words, startled, at the same time reminding herself how untrue things have been this past week.

"We discussed that a long time ago. It was our mutual decision."

A slow nod follows. Daisy isn't convinced that her mother's choice has changed.

"What about now? The entire world knows it. They know about it."

Anxiety reflects Leona Hill's face. Dismay sketches upon her, failing to exaggerate the situation. She breathes in, sips her wine, then rest her hands on the table. The secret she once she knew is unveiled awkwardly.

"So, you knew it."

"No, I discovered it. Now what?"

There's a sense of rigidity felt within the room. Leona stands up from her chair and moves away from her daughter. She fetches her long-lost idea, lost in the oblivion of what she's being convicted of.

"You should go back to your room."

Daisy moves swiftly in silence, though she feels insecure about her future. The reason – her mother's choice, a companion of threat. Her footfalls vibrate as she climbs the staircase. Her memory recalls what she has done in the past – the killing, of course. It's vividly imprinted on her mind. The hotel Grande Albergo delle Palme, that's where she finds herself. Over the last few days, she dimly remembers the face of the murdered Statesman, Blanford Sky. She didn't forget him so easily. However, the long story still remains untouched. The dictator of it, whom she blames – her mother, which she once believed it as a good deed, has now recklessly turned against her. What an odd affair. The discovery makes it so. Besides, Leona Hill is in the frontline assessing a plot for her escape that may eventually cost a life. She doesn't trust her daughter anymore, a bizarre involvement between a daughter and mother. Eighteen-year-old Daisy made a mistake, she thinks now. She shouldn't have obeyed her mother's advice. The man did nothing to her; a crisis creates an illusion of uncertain tragedy around her. It's the affection toward Leona Hill that led her to commit the blunder. And now she's vulnerable because of the person she calls her mother.

She stands stiff before the closed window, watching the beam traverse in the distance. Her index finger taps the window glass as her vision elongates. She feels terrified, but at the same time she gathers her courage. She needs to construct a way out of it. She keeps it a secret, an untold conundrum to herself. Somewhere, a hatch is framing within her, a cage that will protect her from vulnerability. A satirical smile follows out of her, then turns toward her bed. She collects the novel and finds refuge in it again.

"The morning shall smile again," she reads.

CHAPTER TWELVE

At Victim's Door

The city bustles in the early hours. It's not a parade on the busy roads. There's no beat of drums or shrill trumpets from men in uniform. Amidst all the bustling chaos, one can only hear a fair amount of honking and buzzing noise in the city. Ambitious mortals make their way to build their careers in this city of dreams. But for Susan, she had always admired Manhattan as one of her top-prioritized cities to live in. Since her transfer from Chicago, her presence has left marks on every corner of the lanes, from pubs to drug mafias to smugglers. Now she feels quite masterful, sometimes boasting all her expertise to her friend, Massy.

She feels the tinge of light falling on her languid face. She reminds herself about the physical training she never misses. She wakes up, her feet touching the warm floor, as she hears a buzz pitching through the window. She yawns, mouth wide open, and leisurely trails herself to the balcony. The sunbeam hits her directly. She's ready to exercise in her yoga pants. As the day rolls on, she finds herself tired, drenched in sweat. She can't withstand the view and admires it from her sight, then goes back inside to get prepared. She thinks about Leona Hill, the killer, as a suspect, and dials her mother before embarking on her duty.

Of all the crimes in the city, the murder of Blanford Sky had the maximum media coverages across the nation. Nevertheless, many of his peers countered it by portraying the man poorly. But the evidence seems far out of reach. And just like that, Alan's pulse quickens as he walks into the headquarters. He takes a deep breath and follows through the staircase, avoiding the elevator to ensure he doesn't have to wait for it or catch it on the upper floors of the building. He thinks again about the effort to reach the thirteenth floor. On the fourth floor, he waits for the elevator. He presses the button and waits another minute for the doors to open. There are two officers in uniform, a male and a female. Alan stands stiff and still, not looking back at them. A tiny sense of nervousness arises as he waits desperately for the elevator to open, but it's still far up.

"Are you okay?" a voice intimidates him. It's the male officer's tone resonating within the chamber.

"I'm okay," Alan replies, nodding.

"Are you afraid of heights?" the female officer asks.

"No," he responds shortly. He waits for the elevator to reach the thirteenth floor, a desperate sense of urgency emerging in him. The long wait finally shortens. He sees the indicator blink for the thirteenth floor and feels at ease. The elevator halts, the door opens, and a flurry of people wait outside. Alan makes his way out, with the officer following him but in a different direction. Alan drops his ID card that reads his name and address, unaware as he proceeds.

"That's your ID card," says the male officer. His voice cuts through the crowd. Alan turns back, gaping at it.

"Thank you," he says. The officer reads his name. "Nice to meet you, Alan."

"Do you work here?" the female officer questions him.

"No..no," he stutters.

"Have a great day."

"You too."

Alan hastens past the crowd. The door creaks wide open and huge. He walks down the aisle of cabins, past officers, paying no attention, and knocks. It's Susan Kelly's door he's at. He hears a voice calling him in.

"I had hoped to see you," Susan glimmers in the daylight.

"There's something I need to tell you. It might be useful."

She nods. "Go ahead."

His voice shudders at first, then Susan extends a glass of water to him. A terrific tone pops out of him. Weary and fatigued.

"You need to calm down," she says. "Have you walked up the stairs?"

He takes the chair and holds himself steady. Then he reverts to his thoughts.

"It's about the woman. She stays with her daughter on Long Island."

"Are you certain?"

He nods.

"What's the source?" Susan presses.

"I had seen him travel toward Long Island."

"And when was that?"

Alan recalls his memory and his short involvement in the process. Then he makes sure he is right about what he says. He remembers Tony's warning against any deception. This time, he's right about what he thinks.

"A year ago," he mutters.

There's a conflict that triggers him. Some months ago, prior to Blanford Sky's death, a difference of opinion had surfaced which he's aware of. He had heard it across the wall, waiting for the Statesman to be in his chamber. Later, when the dispute toned down, a woman had walked out of the secret anteroom of the chamber, a dreadful expression on her fearful face. She tried to mask herself as she hurried away. She had hidden her sobbing eyes when she sensed the presence of an individual. Alan watched her but failed to recognize the woman. He heard the thud of the door as she hastened away. He waited for the Statesman. Then he heard the footfalls. Blanford wore his coat and fixed his tie. He looked odd, with a queer expression on his face. It was unnerving to look at. He made no judgment about Alan's presence. Instead, he seized a glass and poured wine until the brim flooded. His right hand searched for a cigarette and lit it to take a quick puff.

The assistant stood there, motionless; no gesture movement or order was received to be away. Alan kept quiet and didn't complain. In a few seconds, he felt cigarette fumes spread across the entire wall, blending with its odor.

"What's troubling you now?"

Susan breaks the silence. Then she reverts to her desk. She makes a call to her chief.

"Nothing. It's just the old tale."

"We will make a move now."

"Sure."

Alan gasped. It's the conflict again that makes him weary. He stays silent and shuffles out of the office chamber. He doesn't want to wait anymore and makes his way out of the wide door. The elevator is empty this time, which makes him feel at ease.

No cops to handle. He waits at the entrance of the headquarters. His sight falls onto the streets where the horde assembles. A man addresses the crowd. His voice gets louder as it amplifies. Alan watches and listens keenly. The number increases on the other side of the street. The protest marches on against the failure of the investigation into the murder. Hardly did people know the actual reason why the Statesman was killed. Alan giggles at the crowd.

"What silly support! They fail to see the reality of the man, and think Blanford was a good Statesman," he mutters.

"It's a daily show. Don't bother them."

Susan taps his back. He feels the gut rise upon his spine. Then he breathes in slowly, with an intent he didn't expect.

"You see, the media coverage can change the perception of the case."

"What do you think? Was Blanford Sky a good man?"

"That's a critical question," says Alan.

"It's politics, Alan."

He follows her to the scout, unsure and unaware of what's next or where they were going. His intuition suggests indifferent calculations, then marks upon it tentatively toward Long Island.

"Are we going to arrest her?"

There's a comic smile that emanates from him.

"No, we're going to Blanford Sky's office chamber. It's an investigation."

"But what about the woman?"

Alan tends to assert, for he believes his untold story will surface, putting him in an embarrassing situation, which he has to face in case of any new findings.

"We do as I say," says Susan.

The vanguard, along with the scout career, advances toward the administrative building. It's the city's hustle and bustle that slows them at every turn. The far sightedness doesn't allow her to blink, and she intends to keep it alive for Susan once remembers how the New York Times covered the death story of the Statesman, eventually leading to Broadway for a show. The hoardings and posters still carry the caricature on the streets. Although she attempts to avoid the schema, she can't really take it off, for the message has been covered over the entire street. The caricature still remains the same, with no change – a man in an attempt to rape a woman.

"I heard about that show," says Alan.

"That's pathetic."

The honking stops, and so does their scout. The building stands tall in the middle of the city. This was where the Statesman once held his office. Susan slips out of the vehicle, fixes her hair, then gets her coat. She gets the gun well handle, fastens in the case fix by her haunches. Alan follows her just as he did earlier. He remembers every corner of the building. Some familiar structures and shapes appear before him, though he recognises none. New faces hover around that resemble none of his past. He takes the staircase that once led him to his boss. The perimeter is segregated and no one is allowed to pass through the hallway. The door screeches and footsteps are heard. Susan makes an entry. It has been sealed for a number of days ever since the Statesman was killed. She takes a step forward, scanning the walls that had portraits of the American Civil war. Then her sight falls on the tray, aside from the window. A tea kettle and cups, untouched, lay in sanctity. The hollow room needs enough stuff to make it look occupied. It's a big office room. Her man begins the search. Susan peeks out of the window. The vantage point gives her vivid access to Manhattan's skyline. Right at the edge, she sees the opposite side of Hudson Bay. It appears blue, and the ships make their way to the port. She examines the spots well, then reverts to Alan.

"How does it feel to be back?"

Alan chuckles, walks forth, and lays his back on the edge of the table. "It feels good."

"It's quite a big room."

Susan shuffles toward the desk where Blanford once sat. She examines its edges. Her hands graze through, then she ruminates on the procedure. She makes sure she knows what she's searching for. An evidence in a more precise sense, a concrete one.

"It used to be his work place."

She flashes a definitive smile at the remark. That's exactly what she's looking for. She finds it helpful, and she is even more considerate.

"Thanks for clarifying. I needed to know," she remarks.

She begins her usual engagement, finding all that she can at the desk. Some files and photo frames were untouched for a couple of weeks. The flag stands devoid of the American symbol. She makes it stand on its own two feet. Then her senses guide her to the bulk drawers under the desk, where usually secret treasures are hidden. She opens them one by one, layer by layer, in the hope of finding something major. In the first few she gets nothing, though after that, she's sure she will end up with something strange in her hand. She moves on to the racks on the other side of the desk. This time, it makes her even more confident and convinces her that her search will not go in vain. She finds contraceptive pills, sex toys, a loaded gun, and magazines. She's not amazed by that, but at the same time, it makes her decide – what an astounding discovery! She surfaces it on the desk. The crew handles it as a sort of evidence preserved for further analysis.

"Those strange little toys," she says.

She motions toward Alan, who's six feet away from her vicinity. She has that aura – a smile of endless satisfaction at the new evidence. Alan feels the uproar, and gathering close, abides by the strategic rules to be played upon. He folds his arm.

"It's hard to believe."

"You know a lot more about the man than I do," remarks Susan.

He nods, feeling a disregard for his job. He watches Susan walk away, commanding her crew. Then he finds the moment to unravel his tale.

"I have seen the woman come here quite often."

Susan turns around. She waits to listen to the man before the wrap.

CHAPTER THIRTEEN

At Suspect's Door

Daisy Collins decides to return to Brooklyn. She wants to attend school and meet her friends. She gets a hunch of an awful end, which she dares not imagine. Before she embarks on the coast that noon, she prepares her clothing for the journey ahead. She isn't afraid anymore – neither of the police, nor her mother. An inclination has strained their relationship. Some mornings, mother and daughter scarcely share opinions or see each other. It's the friction of their inexplicable cold war. Both are aware of what's being played over and over. Perhaps Leona Hill might end up imperfectly, that's what Daisy thinks, or vice versa.

She walks to the coast, where the lighthouse keeper looks drenched in the heat. As noon approaches, she feels the warm pebbles hit her bare foot as she leaves footprints on the sandy shore. She watches the keeper hammer nails along the dock. The railing on one side is complete. She enriches herself with the thought of asking about the other night. She fixes a glance at him, watches him work hard, and adds by his side.

"The sea seemed dark last night."

The keeper stops hammering and rests on the wooden dock under the noon light. He cups water from the sea and rinses his face, cooling down.

"I am glad you asked. The lenses weren't perfect. I fixed them this morning. It will shine tonight," he replies.

She nods and inhales deeply as the breeze passes. The waves hit the shore, bringing songs from far away, while ships anchor in the middle of the water. A resonance of unkempt ideas flourishes, making Daisy impatient, for she's here to inform the keeper that she's leaving Long Island soon. She wants her mother to be safe. Somewhere deep down, it's because she still loves her, though love can't be measured.

"Do look after my mother," she mutters in a veiled plea.

It's a shallow hint that keeps the other side at bay. The keeper wonders for a moment, then stops blasting his hammer. He fixes his gaze on her, trying to decipher her motives.

"You probably shouldn't go," he suggests.

She nods. "I hope things will be alright. I need to get back to school."

Daisy stands up and walks away from the dock toward the lighthouse, which once felt like a refuge. She grazes her palm through the stone-carved wall. The keeper joins her.

"You know there's trouble back there."

"It doesn't matter anymore."

Her feet land atop the tower, her gaze streaming through the distant horizon. The ocean water shimmers under the bright, sunny light. Milky clouds hover from the edge, bringing a breeze to the shore. There's a sign of black clouds gathering. She peers as if she might miss the natural occurrence.

"The clouds are bringing rain tonight," she remarks.

The keeper nods, then rests his arm on the tower parapet. He gazes below as the water crashes against the wall.

"I could protect you," he offers.

Daisy peeks at him, sighing softly. "I can protect myself."

"I won't let you go."

"You can't stop me from what I'm about to do."

She descends the footsteps, marching down. The keeper stays behind.

"Could we at least share a meal?" he asks.

"I'll let you know," she replies.

She walks the land, the loose grains of sand nudging her feet, feeling warm. She glances back once, watching the descending sun for her own sake. She takes measured, slow steps. She appreciates the aura and echo of the waves reaching her. She expects the gulls to return to their homes soon, but she can't wait for darkness. She leaves behind the shore, and the lighthouse is yards away. She doesn't turn back, not even a glance. The lighthouse keeper keeps his gaze steady and sharp from atop the tower. Then, she vanishes through the stone wall. He waits for the light to disappear, counting the gulls returning home. And as the ocean changes color from yellow to dark orange, he assembles the lighthouse. He waits for the arrival of the darkness.

A week after the raid at the Statesman's office, a woman arrives at the headquarters. The clock ticks 11 a.m. in the lobby. She appears confused by the décor. The receptionist watches her for several minutes before inquiring about her whereabouts. The woman is alluring in her white and black cut-out dress. She carries a handbag in her right hand as she walks up the staircase in high heels. On the first floor, she waits for the elevator. Her sight lingers on. She peeks at the bunch of flower vase designs as décor throughout the passage. She hears the sound of a tolling bell. The elevator door opens up. Her feet land, and no one can observe her. She searches for the button, the number thirteen.

The door clings, and it moves. The woman stifles and tries hard to breathe. The unrepaired air conditioning creates havoc inside the elevator. She feels the heat rise as well. She closely monitors the floor number. On the thirteenth floor, it halts. The door opens, and she emerges in a rush to breathe in fresh air. The footfalls clamp on the floor as she makes a move. She walks elegantly, confident but tangled in her thoughts compelling. She makes an effort to open the wide door. She finds the structure, the series of cubicles arranged in rows. A small path leads through the aisle. She looks for direction and walks in.

"I'm here to see Detective Susan Kelly."

The woman asks for assistance. She gets the right aid from a lady officer. Her heels march towards Susan's cabin. She knocks at the right door, once, twice, and thrice. She hears the permit tone. She feels the sturdiness as she pushes the door. She keenly observes Susan as she gets closer.

"How may I help you?"

The woman takes the chair and comforts herself.

"I want to know who killed my husband."

"And who is your husband?"

The woman repulses, then rebukes her response. An unjust opinion of what she feels about that. Her pause suggests it.

"It's everywhere in the streets."

For a span of seconds, it causes a hysterical notion. Susan senses it; she gets out of her seat and approaches the woman directly. She knows whom she meant.

"When did you get married to Blanford Sky?"

"A year ago."

She leans on the edge of the table adjacent to the woman.

"Sorry about your loss."

The woman gets fretful, then she remarks on the investigation.

"Aren't you going to do anything? He was an honorable Statesman and a wonderful husband to me."

Susan breathes, then settles herself. A hint of some progress is to be asserted to the woman. She sits back.

"You see, there's a woman who's a suspect."

"A woman?"

It hurts the woman to believe. She feels the wrench drag upon her. Her expression looms. She attempts to reprimand. However, it doesn't happen, though she tries hard.

"We have no idea who she is," says Susan.

"Was he cheating on me?"

"Sorry, we can't comment on that."

The woman in distress stands numb.

"I need to go."

She walks out in a hurry. She senses the displeasure and conceals it within herself. Susan lingers and contemplates the recent discovery. She checks the database and types the Statesman's name. Her intention remains clear. She's still unaware of the woman. The name that she craves. The credentials snap up on her monitor. She scans, line by line. Indeed, an official declaration states the Statesman was married to Julian Baker, a former attorney at Sullivan Cromwell, who is currently serving as a news correspondent for the New York Daily News. Susan keeps it in her memory as she prepares for her untimely errand to Long Island. She plans for the next day and decides to have Alan as a witness. That evening after work, at sundown, she visits her friend's bar, gets the usual drink, and sits along the counter. She doesn't find Alan because it's not Friday, commonly known as the Friday Man. Susan spends more than her usual time until Massy and her brother close the bar. She acts kind and drops them off at their home before she returns to her den. Meanwhile, the night gets chilly and an air of tranquility absorbs the sleeping mortals.

At the early hour of dawn, when the east rays radiate their luster, her alarm bell rings. She can't start her day without the fitness regime. She prepares herself and fits into her routine. Susan makes a call to her mother when the day light falls on the hard turf. Shadows overcast hers, they're the skyscrapers that make a silhouette and stretch over a long, endless space. She's ready to make a move on her sturdy investigation. But what suggests her is the unnerving discovery of Julian Baker, a widow, who seems so mysterious and odd at the same time. It's just the beginning of a long history to unfold. The untold narrative is to be unleashed in many unfavorable ways.

That morning, she meets Alan at the headquarters building. The inquiries are authentic. There is no hard chase to find the actuals. The procedures must be fulfilled for an accurate path. She turns her chair toward the anxious man, Alan.

"You didn't know about Julian Baker. How am I supposed to believe that?"

"Blanford Sky was a secret man. He never disclosed his personal life to anyone, not even to the media. Julian Baker is a new term for me."

She nods. "They were married a year ago."

Alan folds his arm and stands steady as he makes it clear to himself. "It could be possible."

"We will move immediately."

The scouts wait outside the building as they assemble and prepare. Tony has words for Susan, some guidance for the inquiries. He makes sure the suspects do not get to know about their arrival. It's just a formal interrogation, no pressure, he suggests.

"Make it easy," he says.

Susan nods. Alan watches her as she walks into her car.

"Have you ever shot a person?" Alan asked promptly.

"You see, this thing I'm carrying on my haunches is not a toy."

"Tough girl, huh!"

She looks at him with a playful, smouldering expression. The scout leaves for Long Island.

"Why did you choose to join the police?" it pops up from Alan.

"It's a long story, Alan. I'll share it with you over a Friday beer. How about that?"

He smirks.

An hour later, they find themselves on the Isle. Susan checks the GPS system over and over again. She doesn't want to get misled. She wants to find an accurate location. It directs them along the long coast road. The Atlantic seems to be rough and windy. Rows of residences dash along the coast. Her sight falls on the far, distant lighthouse. The glimmering rays overcast the blue sky. Gulls begin to squeak in the open air with their wings wide spread. The swells roar, lapping the shore a hundred times.

"Alright, this is it," she says.

The keeper views them from a distance. An officer walks up to him only to ensure that they were in the right place. He asks to be more certain.

"That's the house."

He nods, stunned and unable to react quickly. A sort of fear creeps into him. A wrong cause is on its way. The keeper stays silent and watches the officer report. Susan and her team get on their feet and feel the ocean breeze immediately. His vision lengthens, then he rambles toward the stone wall. The porch appears green and decorative. Up ahead, some feet away, the shiny white door awaits a welcome knock. Susan stops at the steps. She wanted to make the first strike. Once, twice, thrice, and then fourth time. The response delays. She taps again, comparatively louder. It unlocks from the other side and widens. A woman appears in her body-con attire.

"Yes," she says. "How may I help you?"

"Leona Hill, right?"

She nods. Her sheer expression suggests pretence.

"We are from the New York State Police Department. We have some inquiries to be conducted," states Susan.

"Sure, go ahead."

Leona directs them to the kitchen table, where she pauses and sits quite well. Confident, assertive, and well versed is what she assures herself.

The questioning begins.

CHAPTER FOURTEEN

The Meet Hour

Susan scans the house, the walls, and the pictures dangling on them. A speculation mounts on her. She reads the photographs well, then redirects at her. Her men stand aside, none in action. The necessary pursuit has been achieved. She gets closer to the kitchen table, where Leona has her hand fiddling in nervousness.

"Who's that man in the photograph?"

"That's my late husband."

"Was he a lighthouse keeper?" Susan queries.

She stretches her neck to peep at the lighthouse from the window. She finds the structure similar. It's the same, she reads for herself. She takes a seat and clears her throat in front of the defendant. The queries are to be poured until they reach a clear conclusion. She utters one after another with roots that tangle upon the truth. Susan mingles in the process.

"There's chaos in the city about the murder of a Statesman, and I'm certain you're aware of that."

Leona, the defendant, nods certainly. She keeps it slow and steady, and she measures with confidence what she exhibits.

"I'm aware of it, and what's your point?"

"You see, there's a woman who takes your name. She believes it has something to do with you. You can't pretend to forget Julian Baker, right?"

Leona corners her vision at Alan. She perceives him with judgment in her eyes. She senses that it's through him that they got here. If she remembers correctly, she had seen him at Blanford's office once.

"You're doing the wrong thing, officer. I don't know any Julian Baker."

Susan titters, then gets out of her posture. She dawdles around the kitchen corner. She picks up a glass for herself and fills it with water to quench her thirst. She resumes her interrogation at ease.

"Fair enough. I hope the woman is mistaken."

"There is nothing to find here. You're in the wrong place."

She gets off her chair and walks toward the door. "Please, excuse me. I have work to do."

"Thank you for your time," says Susan.

The door is opened, and the team walks out. Susan follows last.

"We'll see you again," she says.

"That won't be necessary."

"I highly doubt that."

Alan waits for her at the scout. She takes a keen look at the surroundings, then her feet marches toward the crew. Up ahead, she sees a figure approaching closer. Daisy Collins slows her pace as she encounters Susan. She breathes, appears confident, and adds elegance to her outlook. In her mind, she still thinks she's undiscoverable for her crime. She halts as they exchange pleasantries.

"You must be Leona's daughter."

"Yes."

"Well, nice to meet you."

Daisy doesn't question much. She's cautious and alert mentally.

"I've got to go. My mother is waiting."

"Sure. I hope you had a great time at the coast."

She nods and paces again.

"Why didn't you arrest her?" Alan probes.

"I know about the bounty and the posters, my friend. It's just that I want to know the truth of all this mess." Susan assures.

Susan meets her team members. She speculates on the entire dubious play of narration, then remarks on the utter disappointment of what she had not expected. She claims the woman is cunning and wisely manipulative in her concerns. However, the twist is yet to be discovered and unearthed from the deepening mystery evolving in the case. Before she gets inside the scout, her vision elongates toward the coast. The lighthouse appears larger and brighter from a close shot. She rolls her eyes in every direction and points at the keeper. The keeper, employed and engaged, is oblivious. He fixes a three foot notice at the edge of the coast, where water keeps lapping hundreds of times a day. It says, *please avoid going into the deep; the ocean is rough*, a warning for visitors. Just then, she feels the hint of someone standing next to her. Alan clears his throat in haste.

"Any foul play by the keeper?"

"We don't know yet, Alan. We can't let escape every suspect. We will find out," she says.

They return to the city.

At quarter past three, Susan Kelly knocks on Tony's door. He looks tempted to hear about the progress. However, the long run isn't in her hands. She finds it hard to elaborate on the entire tale and rephrases it in a way that should sound compelling. The attention seeks Tony; his ears open, and he escalates his mind over the scenario. A surprising detail unfurls that brings his spines into an erect position on his chair.

"So, you're saying Blanford Sky was a married man."

She nods her head, assuring her findings aren't wrong with concrete evidence to support them. Until now, it's just a story for Tony, and when the evidence was presented to him, his head came into play.

"Julian Baker is her name, a former attorney at Sullivan Cromwell," she says.

She gives her earlier details about the woman and her visit to her office regarding the investigation. Tony examines her photograph and stares keenly at Julian Baker. He finds her ID card hung over her neck, which says her name and the law firm she was associated with. Then he shifts his body, gets on his feet, and fetches two cups of tea. On his desk rests the print bulletin, The New York Times. He sips and offers one to her. Then he gets back onto his chair. Tony picks up the newspaper and urges her.

"You should see this."

The headline reads, *Shootout at Broadway*. The entire city knew about the incident, and theatres were at a halt. People were scared and frightened.

"What's the show?"

"You know better," says Tony.

"Again."

Susan reads the words, line by line and finds fault in how The New York Times deliberately plays politics in a matter that isn't supposed to be disclosed to common people.

"Is the actor alive?"

"He must be in a critical condition," adds Tony.

She sets the paper on the desk and sighs. An expression of disappointment shows up on her expressions; she meddles along with it, finding it gruesome and acting quite confident to not leave the guilty.

Not long ago, the Broadway was the centre of attention for people with artistic skills, the portrayal of their life's work and the talents where each one avails the first opportunity to become a public figure. It was where dreams found their way. Now it's just a platform of risk and death. What went wrong on the day of the show? A mere question of excellence surfaced, with posh people asking for security. It's the business of the show that drives people of uncommon interests to Broadway, hoping to find entertainment that can be praised for ages. But this shootout is different, linking to previous instances; this time, it craves a more emotional and sentimental touch. It needs to be dealt with fundamentally from the root, and the chaos has been unnerving. The noon has been a curse for the showgoers. As the chaotic crowd erupts at the juncture of the road, Tony finds himself surrounded by angry faces and fearful souls, begging for protection. The killing has been done. The actor has been slain on the stage, blood dripping from his wounds. His last breath lingers as he strives to live.

Tony takes hold of the situation. His men safeguard the rest and evacuate quickly. The siren wails outside, the ambulance whines and the actor is laid out and taken to the hospital. For an hour, the clueless scene hovers, and the streets stand empty and barren. Tony walks out of the theater, twitching his head in all possible directions.

"Seal the hall," he commands.

Then his feet move forward, and he raises his head in the smouldering noon. A massive banner hangs over the entrance at the top, a display of the drama, depicting a woman being raped and a man being stabbed in the heart.

"That's really gross. The show must be banned," muttered Tony.

While the streets appear deserted within an hour, a few in the vicinity had witnessed the terrible occurrence. The other theatres continued their business for the rest of the day. Tony and his team leave and vacate the place within the next few minutes.

Susan listens attentively. She can't digest what she heard about the man but avails herself in the time of need as a member of the case. She sounds curious and eccentric about the matter, involving herself in a way that might help contributing facts. Her gestures suggest this, and the sheer expression on her face confirms it.

"What's the update?" she asks.

Tony breathes out, then leans back on his chair. "Yet to record a statement from the victim. It's supposed to be today."

"What about the shooter, the accused?"

"It's an underground gang; mostly drug and sex peddlers. What surprises me is that these people are all illegal immigrants from Mexico. According to intelligence, they reside somewhere on the coast side."

"Any idea who funds them or who the boss is?"

Tony laughs briefly, then gets off his chair and fetches a glass of water for himself. He remains silent for a few seconds, then he remarks on the existing facts, which startle him in an odd manner. He leans on his desk, arms crossed.

"Blanford Sky."

For Susan, the name is not new. Somewhere in the back of her mind, she knew it would come up. Her intuition was right. Her eyebrow raises at the name. Taken aback by the unanticipated revelation, she now faces a massive conundrum. The challenge is real.

"Wow! This is hell," she blurts, "What's the source?"

"Well, the FBI intelligence can't go wrong," adds Tony.

"That's why those criminals were trying to protect the image of the Statesman."

"And that's the reason why they shot the actor who played Blanford Sky. And only at that theatre."

These new findings about the Statesman had remained in oblivion for years, as no one anticipated the rackets being carried out for political gains and power. The erstwhile Statesman happened to be the leader of a pack involved in drug and sex peddling worldwide. It's a big business out there; no matter how illegal it may be termed, with money and power it's all legal to showcase superiority.

Tony departs from the headquarters as the sun descends below the horizon. The fading twilight disperses and dissolves into the waning darkness, and his presence remains absent. He didn't forget about the actor and evinces his honesty in his duty, an officer who savors appreciation from others. Before he leaves, he ensures the urgency and Susan Kelly reciprocates his act of taking charge. She watches him from her window. The thirteenth floor is quite high up in the sky, and every object appears tiny. She discerns no difference between the vehicles, but the wailing siren stands out. That's Tony. She breaks into a lofty smile and dashes out of the workroom. She peeks at the wall clock and reads half past seven. Once more, she decides to summon Julian

Baker, a routine task pending and unresolved. She writes it on a sticky note as reminder, and taps it on the monitor screen, and walks out. She heads to the bar, a customary tradition, and meets her friend Massy Paul. However, it's not Friday and her hope of encountering Alan diminishes.

Broadway has since prohibited the show of the slain Statesman.

CHAPTER FIFTEEN

Blanford Sky's Step to State's Senate

In 1985, young nineteen-year-old Blanford Sky graduates from school. The only photograph with his mother he shares is framed in his bedroom. The struggle is real as he watches his mother fight for survival each day. She can't afford anymore for him anymore – education and the bills. The debt remains unpaid, with claims pouring in from all sides. Sometimes the threats were real. On days when they ran short of cash, altercations seemed inevitable between them.

"Why are you making it hard for me?" she yells.

Blanford's mother is jaded and weary. She feels disappointment lingering upon her, vexed at everything about her son.

"What do you want me to do?" Blanford replies.

At dinner, it has become a customary drill, jeopardizing each other for all causes and undone tasks that have never been in their favor. Blanford leaves the table in an argument. His mother watches him as he dashes out of the door with a screeching thud. She feels sorry about him, her voice not loud, diminishing and failing to stop him. She sits and sighs, a restless mother shedding tears for her better days of the past. It is difficult for her to manage her son's irreverent youth that seems far away, and she counts on the hope of changes to come. She craves to retain empty expectations. She gazes at the door again, anticipating her son's return, but it's a hollow dream. Eventually, she has to give up, and watch the darkness as the night soars in a silent attempt at calmness.

Blanford doesn't return until the next morning. His mother hunts for him among the neighbors, but it is in vain. In melancholic plight, she returns. She watches the sun descend as her feet rest on the steps of her front door. She rests herself and gazes at the fading daylight. She feels regretful; how unpersuasive she was in not being able to stop her son from absconding. She rests her forehead on her arm and glares at the coast, the lapping waves returning without fail. The Atlantic oceanfront changes its color from orange to yellow as the twilight grazes upon it. The South Shore appears panoramic of the Island. It's been their home since they moved from Maine to Long Island.

Blanford never shared good terms with his father. On the day his father expired, he didn't attend the funeral service. A month later, he and his mother moved to Long Island, leaving their past behind and never remembering him.

The fret seems real now. She glances at the clock again. It ticks ten p.m. The dinner table remains as it is, holding on with the desire for her son's return. And as time passes, it yields nothing but loneliness that encages her. Her surroundings are silent, and the neighbor's light go off. It will be another night without Blanford at home. She rests on the steps of her front door, the roars from the oceanfront distinctly rhythmic, and her sight pulsates back and forth in the neighborhood. Lately, the feeling of exhaustion overwhelms her and forces her to go inside. She's frightened, afraid of the wrong impression she has about her son. The night gets tougher and tougher for her to endure. She falls asleep on her couch in the living room. The television murmurs, its light flickering in the dark room. She lets it continue to wipe away her fear and fill her ears with sound. She escapes the night in her ardent yearning and allows herself to rely on her faith.

When the morning light falls on her, she wakes up with a thought to be true to herself and finds herself engaged in tasks. She walks around the neighborhood, greeting familiar faces, hoping somewhere that her son will return. Soon, this chore will end for her. A week later, she gets a job she had applied for before her son left. Now, with a reminiscent impression and feelings about her son, she begins to show up each day to rebuild herself. A week later, on her return from work, she gets a call. The voice is familiar and sensitive. She walks the pavement of her neighborhood, heading home. Up ahead, some miles away, the lighthouse stands rigid. The twilight fades on the distant horizon. Her footfalls halts in front of her door. She can still hear the voice on the phone.

"Blanford, is it you?"

"Hey Mom."

"Where have you been, son?"

"Not far. I'm doing good, mother. I got a job."

She feels elated by the news. She breaks into a simple smile and trudges inside.

"Good. I'm proud of you."

A silence builds for a few seconds before Blanford breaks it. He's sensitive and regretful for leaving home and hurting his mother.

"I'm sorry for being a bad son, Mom."

Her eyes fill with tears. She clears her throat and sits on the couch. She grabs a bundle of napkins and rubs her eyes. Then she settles for the conversation.

"When can I see you?"

A pause follows from the other end. It's the hiss of breath that relays into her ear. Blanford goes silent for a while, then reverts.

"I'll let you know. I have to go now," he says and drops the receiver.

The sound goes silent and blunt. The darkness turns tender, and a soft breeze sets in. She goes to the kitchen to prepare her last meal.

Blanford Sky meets his old school friend, a Mexican by race. It's his friend who assists him in getting a job that pays well. In time, Blanford learns about the business and becomes an expert in his position. Most of his workmates turn out to be Mexican, many of them illegal immigrants dwelling along the South Bay of the Island. He has become an important dealer in the business by the end of six months. He hasn't called his mother, nor has she called him. Now he operates the entire South Bay, handling everything from stocking to selling to finding clients. He has begun to deal in drugs. Most of the suppliers are from Mexico, landing across the bay via the Atlantic Ocean. He helps them stock the goods on the shore and then delivers them to the highest-paying buyers. From there, the products spread to various clubs and bars through different channels and customers. It's a big business that pays him well, and Blanford starts to get rich. He allows boat and ships to land and make space for them at the dockyard along the coast, which he secretly operates.

Delving deeper into the trade, it becomes apparent that not just ordinary men are involved. Powerful people, including politicians, are the main beneficiaries. This illegal activity, unknown and unverified on many levels, allow politicians of the country to go uncharted, leading to the rise of the business into the mainstream. It's a win-win situation for both parties. Blanford's seizes every opportunity to expand his associations. He gets a big share of the money that comes in, and remains diligent in his duties. It's a risky but well-channeled path with connections from lawmakers to suppliers.

Nine months later, Blanford calls his mother. He agrees to see her. He gets a sedan and drives toward his home. The fading daylight beams from the distant horizon, and the coast, as usual, laps with waves. As the daylight ends, the signal arrives from the corner lighthouse miles away with a powerful beam stretching across the shore. He sees the changes – the white picket fences bordering the house. The sedan comes to a stop. Blanford gets out of the car with a low thud of the door. He walks toward the mailbox at the entrance of the house, unhooks it, and slides his hand to grab a few envelopes. Then his feet march through the porch.

Inside, his mother hears the sound of the car arriving from the window. She draws the curtain aside and sees her son. Her face lights up with joy, and her laments disappear in a moment. The knock reaches her ears and she hastens to unlock the door. She stands motionless, finding herself in deep melancholic gratification at seeing her son.

"Mom," says Blanford.

His arms open wide for an embrace. He feels how crucial this moment is and then finds his mother sobbing. She wipes her teary eyes and clears her throat, breaking the silence with a quivering tone.

"I'm glad you came to see me."

The blissful night is rewarding as they share dinner together. Blanford stays the night and spends time with his mother, talking about his business, only the fine parts. He tells how he meets state politicians through his work. Their long prattle continues until the deep night falls silent, accompanied by the ongoing rhythm of the oceanfront. The whizz of the splash brings a cool breeze from the coast, and miles apart, the glow of the lighthouse ascends its beam, mapping out the night sky. His mother retreats to her room to rest for the night and falls asleep. She has to go to work the next day, a reminder that lingers.

Before Blanford leaves, he shares one last breakfast with his mother and then drops her off at her workplace. Her voice sounds timid and apprehensive as she speaks.

"Be back soon."

A smile spreads across her face, a pleasant and courteous gesture.

"I had a great time, Mother. See you soon," he says as he drives the sedan away.

She watches him take the turn and nearly trips onto the floor as she tries to enter the building. She balances herself, takes control, and as usual, the day goes on.

Back in the business, Blanford takes an assignment to expand the area of operation. He visits the eastern stretch of the Island. His visits marks him with a well-end, where he gets to meet a man who works as a lighthouse keeper. Fritz Collins has been working as a keeper for a decade now, dwelling with his family in the eastern side of the Island, enduring the roughness of the coastline. The sedan drives evenly along the flat track, rattling with cobblestones beneath the tires. Behind follows the dusty strands of grime, weaving the track. He pulls the brake skillfully and comes to a halt. Few feet away, Fritz Collins stands with a rope in his hand, deciphering the elegant man wearing shades. Overhead, the sunny sky chimes with the breeze from the farthest Atlantic. Blanford walks forward and peers around. The lighthouse stands huge and sturdy at the bottom, with its strength visible from the sight.

"How can I help you, sir?" asks Fritz.

"Are you the keeper?"

Fritz nods and waits for Blanford's words.

"I'm Blanford Sky."

"Fritz Collins."

"I have an offer for you. It's a good deal."

Fritz gapes at his face for a few seconds, unanticipated and abrupt, unable to comprehend. Never before has anyone approached him in such a manner.

"What's the point?"

"You see, it's a business. I can make you rich. All I need is a partner," adds Blanford Sky.

"But how can I trust you?"

Blanford sighs and leans back on the hood of the sedan. He takes a cigar out of his pocket, lights it instantly, and puffs the smoke into the air.

"You aren't losing anything," he says.

He sets himself to leave, unlatching his car door and about to set his feet inside.

"Hold on."

The voice is quite needy and fascinating. Blanford turns back and drops his half-burned cigar. A gentle nod follows. He gets called below the attic of the lighthouse. He makes a gentle entry through the narrow staircase. It feels damp as he runs his palm along the texture of the stone wall. Fritz lights a candle.

The business talk begins, and the listener draws an attention, finding the fascinating narration delightful. The money and the job are both at stake, whilst Fritz has already made up his mind. He needs money and is keen to work for the man. Thirty minutes later, Blanford steps out of the attic and dashes away in his sedan. The slanting beams from the day's end reveal the shadow lengthening as the keeper watches him accelerate. He dreams of a car and a big house. It's a lot of money, Fritz thinks, as he picks up the hammer to fix the nail at the dock. He works until darkness engulfs the shore.

In a week, he gets into the business and begins to accomplish what he dreamt of. He allows the shore to be used for the boats that arrive from distant Atlantic locations. In time, his attic turns into a stockroom. The smuggling is real, as he imagines himself directing fellow peers toward the attic. Heavy boxes of illegal packets containing drugs and money flows through him. Occasionally, he finds attractive, good-looking random ladies landing at his attic. It's a part of the business, Blanford explains to him.

"It's for the State politicians. It's called seduction."

"Are you running for President?" Fritz heckles. "A bonus is needed."

"You will have your share, my friend," says Blanford Sky.

He lights a cigarette and watches the sun descending as the unloading finishes. He offers a piece of his collection to Fritz Collins, who joins him. The dock allows them a vantage sight of the horizon. As darkness envelops, Fritz prepares the lens at the top of the lighthouse. He waits for the man to camp out, then wades to the top of the tower where the lens is fixed. The faint darkness arrives, and Fritz presses the button. Its beam elongates in the distance, and he watches the sedan from his vantage point racing away. He waves at Blanford, who sees from his rearview mirror and gestures back. Fritz spends another hour before he returns home.

A week later, Blanford Sky shows up. For the first time, he's been invited to Fritz's house. That's where the erstwhile Statesman meets Leona Hill and learns about their daughter, Daisy Collins. He brings a cheque book that renders the amount Fritz is supposed to receive. The deal gets done, and the money is paid. Blanford shares dinner with the family. In the backyard, an orchard is being raised, which comes to the man's notice. The climbers spread their tendrils across the wooden white-colored fence.

"You are a wine man," says Blanford.

He gets off his chair and lumbers to the back door into the open space, where the vineyard smells out in the freshly moonlit night. He touches the leaves and takes them closer to his nostrils. Then nods his head.

"It's pure," adds Fritz.

"I don't doubt you."

Blanford Sky vacates himself for the night, as Fritz and his family watch him drive the sedan in the fading light. Then, at the turn, he vanishes from their sight. Daisy sighs before she walks inside the house. She senses guilt in the man, an unclear intention. A teenage mind leads her to conclude about the man.

From New York to California, the trade escalates. Blanford Sky is now a renowned man and a spoken personality amongst the community. Well in touch with eminent politicians in the State, he's been granted a chance to run for the State Senate. The next few years, he amuses the horde, rallying across the New York State. Money and power certainly did not abandon him. In years, he made more from the illegitimate business. On the day he is sworn in as a member of the State Senate, his invitation doesn't go to waste from the Fritz family. However, the absence of his mother disheartens him as he spoke those words over the dice for the horde before commencing his office. Three days later, he makes a visit. His speech has been broadcasted over the entire New York State, which his mother didn't fail to hear from her vintage television set.

However, after he took office in the State Senate, he ran the business covertly along with its stakeholders. As time passed, his voice and words began to dominate the political scenario. His speeches tempted crowds, luring ears, and in moderate affairs, his progress influenced his adherents. Many joined later, and the speech that made him the conqueror, the Statesman, was when he talked about Black deprivation, which churned the nation. People heard him as the good, the honest, the loyal and the trustable commander, a Statesman, as they said. The New Yorker had him on their cover page, and The New York Times glorified him with the headline *A Statesman is Born, Listen to Him.*

CHAPTER SIXTEEN

Suite No.13, Hotel Grande Albergo delle Palme Re-opens

It's a rainy day when an old man stands with his umbrella unfurled among the droplets. Reporters surround him as he marches toward the hotel. A correspondent asks him about his stay. He has booked room number thirteen, the suite.

"Are you going to stay in the murdered room?"

He ceases his steps and responds in a French accent.

"Of course."

"Aren't you afraid?"

He avoids the question and follows his escorts. He is guided by the bellman along with his luggage. Before he sets foot in the elevator, he receives amiable greetings from the receptionist. The key is handed over to him. The old french man treads toward the elevator. The bellman stands behind him as the doors close. On the fourth floor, he appears again. He allows the bellman to lead, hands him the key, and waits outside before unlocking the door. The suite appears indifferent, distinct from what previous residents had known. The old man smells French roses with a calming scent of jasmine as he strides in. The bellman explains him the décor and the conveniences. The bedrooms are adorned with distinct art from the medieval period, which interests the old man. He keeps his lingering gaze on the walls hanging with paintings and art. He then reaches the tea table, where a jar of cookies and biscuits are kept for him. Stacks of saucers lie on top of the rack. His hand runs through the clay teapot, sensing its warmth.

"Thank you for your guidance," the old man says.

He bestows some dollars to the bellman and allows him to exit. The old man advances and pours some tea from the clay teapot. He then shifts toward the window. He peeks at his pocket watch from the left pocket; it reads 11:00 hrs. The rain hasn't stopped yet. He stands close to the window edge, gazing outside as he enjoys his tea. He lingers in his thoughts about how his old friend got murdered, leaving behind a secret that he's here to discover. He thinks about the documented classified schema, an unexecuted mission. The conundrum prevails in the hands of the Statesman's partner, who will soon respond to the cause of the blueprint schema that everybody is looking for. Just then, he hears a knock. It's the new bellboy who arrives with the servings, a customary courtesy for every new guest. The old man's imagination ceases. He sees the young boy drop the servings on the table.

"What's your name?" the old man asks.

"Arthur, Sir."

"Tell me, what's the best theatre show in New York?"

"I do not know, sir."

Arthur sounds humble. His modesty is tested. His hands quiver as he holds the tray. He prepares to leave.

"What about the slain Stateman's show?"

"To my knowledge, sir, Broadway has been closed ever since the shootout. Please excuse me," says Arthur.

The old French man makes him wait for another minute as he reaches into his pocket. He pulls out a dollar bill and hands it to the bellboy.

"Here's your earning."

Arthur hesitates at first, but then feels the urge and fills his pocket with the bill.

"Thank you, sir."

He shuts the door, leaving the old man in privacy.

At dusk, the old man takes a walk along the Broadway street. He glances at his pocket watch, keeping himself in line. He smokes a pipe, an inevitable necessity to disguise his appearance. His effort to look like an American is admirable. He speaks less to avoid revealing his French accent and blends in with the crowd. He has named himself Rufus Young, a name in stark contrast to his old age. The surname 'Young' is predominantly inapt for his appearance. His footfalls halt at the theatre entrance. His sight fixes on the shut door. The display hoarding glows brightly, casting his shadow on the street turf. The rain has washed away the dust; it's a surreal and clumsy day. He finds people in every corner – the restaurants, the bars, and some gaming houses in focus. He wears a hat and coat for protection against the cold wind after the shower. Rufus imagines the aftermath of the shootout, with strict legislation imposed on the show business. He looks across the street. A car splashes water onto him, the result of irregular pits on the road after the rainfall. Rufus shouts at the driver, who pays no heed. He manages to dust off his coat and crosses the street in search of a bar.

He reads the label and ascends a few steps. The keeper opens the door for him.

"Welcome to Black Swan, sire."

Rufus sails in, and the impression gives him a vivid remembrance of his favorite club in Paris. He feels swayed and less elated about the place. He misses the décor of the French reverie. He nods as he passes people and smokes his pipe as well. At the counter, he receives greetings from the bartender, a glamorous woman, often called a ladies' man.

"What can I serve you, sire?" she says.

"Anything would do."

"Well, I will give you the best drink ever here on Broadway."

Rufus scans around over her shoulder and finds couples kissing at the remote end. He listens to the music in the background, then opts to take a seat at the counter.

"Here's your Manhattan coupe, sire, the best in the city."

"Thank you, I appreciate it."

"If you need anything else, I'm here."

"You're beautiful," Rufus gestures.

He spends the night in solitary repose in his suite. He gets his dinner served and later takes a walk with his newly made friend, Arthur. His pocket watch reminds him of his tired day, and he shortens the walk in the hotel garden.

"Thank you, Arthur, for joining me on my walk."

"At your service always."

"Goodnight."

The phone rings in suite no. thirteen. Rufus watches the beam infiltrating through the window. The clock ticks nine. He pours some tea and stands aside the frame, watching the kids play in the garden. Twice, thrice, he pays no heed regardless of its urgency. The call continues. Eventually, his attention is diverted, and he answers the receiver. His voice sounds bristly. He hears from the other end; it's the hotel receptionist. He settles his robe and listens to the voice.

"Sire, there's a lady officer who would like to meet you."

"I'm not aware of any," he says.

"She says it's urgent."

"Send her in."

Rufus clears his throat and sips the last portion of his tea. He waits for the lady officer. He grumbles to himself, walks back and forth, ties his robe tight at his waist, and sits anxiously. He cranes his neck, waiting for the knock at the door. He lights his pipe and attempts to stay composed. Then his prayer are answered, and he hears the knock at the door. Rufus waits for another round, making sure he hears it clear and sharp. He hangs onto his residual confidence on his last puff.

"Come in, it's open."

Footsteps tap the floor as they reach deeper inside the suite.

"Hello! Mr. Rufus."

The voice resonates as Susan Kelly finds him seated in his wingback chair, smoking a pipe. She gets closer and finds the vicinity filled with artefacts. The room has been remodeled; she perceives the difference. She then leans on a table, arms crossed.

"I'm not sure who you are."

"Right. I'm Detective Susan Kelly from NYPD. I'm here on purpose."

Rufus exhales streams of smoke from his pipe, then breathes deeply. His leg is crossed over the other. He leans back and makes eye contact with the detective.

"And what's the purpose?"

"How did you know about this suite?"

He titters and walks over to the tea table. Grabbing two cups, he seizes the moment and pours tea into both.

"Tea."

"Thank you," says Susan.

"I'm French. I have sources all around."

Susan sips her tea and pipes her queries. "So, you knew Blanford Sky, right?"

"You caught me. We were business partners."

"What kind of business?"

The old man walks toward the window. He envisions the rainy day and then turns. Behind him, Susan remains fixed, a feet away.

"I suppose that's none of your purpose," Rufus says with a very French tone.

She nods, a gesture to assure him she doesn't find him guilty of a crime. "What brought you here?"

"We had an incomplete deal, a pact among the partners."

"What is it about?"

"I hope your purpose is done. Now, if you may excuse me, I have to go for a walk," says Rufus Young.

Susan exits without another word and watches the old man take the elevator. A skeptical intuition surges as she makes her way out of hotel Grande Albergo delle Palme. She finds that Rufus Young has already become a rumor among the press. The mystery of his choosing suite no. thirteen haunts her. She wastes no time and returns to headquarters. On her way, she encounters Alan, picks him up, and shares the details about the old french man.

A week later, a disarray erupts. Rufus Young goes missing. His absence alarms the hotel crew. His return is still awaited. Suite no. thirteen remains on standby as the man has not checked out from the hotel Grande Albergo delle Palme. The chaos stirs the press, *the mysterious man goes missing*, prints the headlines again. The name of the French old man is disclosed; Rufus Young makes the New York Times again, this time for a real reason – his missing case.

Susan reads it at her desk on a catastrophic morning. The fault lies in misjudging the man during her visit. Helpless and stagnant in finding the real reason for his visit, she laments. She grabs the paper and proceeds to Tony's chamber. The discussion is lengthy and utterly rigid as both see the lack of confidence in their methods.

"He talked about an incomplete deal, a kind of pact. A beneficiary of Blanford Sky," says Susan.

"Make a visit to Long Island. I'm certain Leona Hill knows something about the missing Frenchman. And summon Julian Baker to my office immediately."

When the sun ascends overhead, Susan departs from the chaos of the city. During her hour-long drive, she engages herself in her thoughts and the strategic implementation she needs to put through. Yet, it weighs heavily on her to solve the mysterious case. She gets Alan in her front seat and debates over Rufus Young. It gets complicated as they seek to understand. The lengthy coast appears in the shimmering shine of the bright sunny day. The south shore stretches for miles. They are quick with their motive, knowing how crucial it is. Susan stops her car at a road that leads to the lighthouse. A feet away, she sees the white picket fence and the stone wall guarding the house. She decides to make a move toward the shore. The dunes glitter and shine with tiny mixed pebbles of quartz. She feels her feet sink as they walk through. No one is in sight for now. She instructs Alan to look round. They wait in the scorching heat. A while later, the keeper arrives from the opposite end. He holds a bucket in the right and a fishing rod rests on his shoulder. He opens the attic and notices their presence near the dock waterfront.

"How can I help you?" his voice fades.

Susan turns around and finds herself amazed. "Great, I'm looking for you."

The keeper stands quietly, allowing himself to be a part of the conversation. He waits for the real purpose.

"Have you seen an old man come to that house?" she adds, pointing toward the house.

The keeper flickers and twitches, a nervous expression surging on his face, but he tries to maintain his composure.

"No, I have not seen any old man."

The air rises from the oceanfront and chills across the coast. Just as they were about to leave, the attic door creaks, not from the wind, but from a hand pulling it. The appearance seems familiar. Leona Hill walks out of the hollow room, resurfacing into the bright open space.

"That's Leona Hill," says Susan. "What's she doing here?"

From her vantage sight, she moves forward, making her way quickly. She ignores the detective, but is intercepted as Susan stops her on the way. A series of questions follows rapidly, with uncertain answers. Leona denies the appearance of Rufus Young. While the probing continues, Alan finds something strange around the corner, quite far from the lighthouse. The bump is covered with dunes and a cross is fixed on top – a grave, to be more precise. Intuition remains alert as suspicion of foul play urges the detective to investigate. They rush to the spot. The grave appears fresh, newly covered with dirt on the surface. A nameless mound lies before them.

"That's my uncle's grave," says the keeper.

Susan glares at him, her skepticism evident.

"When did this happen?"

Leona stands aside, speechless, mute.

"Two days ago."

She skips the rest of the debate. However, it bothers her that Leona's daughter isn't at home.

"Well, we shall meet again," Susan says as she exits the coast.

She observes keenly, examining the house before they move back to the city. The evidence has been omitted all along the search and she's certain that the lighthouse keeper and Leona Hill have a substantial role in the heinous act. Alan drives on their return, while she sits in the front seat. She gazes at the stretching oceanfront as the sun goes down. The color changes from orange to yellow along the thin line of separation on the far horizon.

Rufus Young exchanges words with the hotel receptionist prior to his visit to Long Island. He keeps it short and precise. He warns about his absence for the day and assures his return the next day. The suite isn't empty as of now. The old French man holds his umbrella and a briefcase as he walks out of the entrance. A taxi arrives and halts right on the spot. The arrangement has been made. He hurries that morning. For the first time, the man leaves the city's vicinity. The long road ends in the coastal town of Long Island. He sees the lighthouse from a distance and walks ahead with the umbrella. The breeze heckles at times, but he manages to stay firm by the handle. The umbrella hood protects him from the heat.

At the dock, the keeper notices him and inquires about his whereabouts. Rufus discloses his intention to meet Leona. He follows the keeper toward the white picket house. He sees the stone wall on the other side of the boundary. The door gets a knock. Rufus stands behind the keeper and scans around the yard.

"He's here," says the keeper.

The door is half-open.

"Send him in," says Leona, "and you wait outside."

Rufus enters. There's no significant greeting, as though they knew each other. It is a formality of no choice, but on a certain day, the fate is about to change.

"It's pleasant to see you again, Rufus."

"I'm here for the chronicle that Blanford left behind."

An undeniable gesture erupts from the woman. She describes the non-existence of such a chronicle left by her husband. Leona disagrees with the old French visitor.

"There's nothing like that."

"What about the deal of assassination?"

She stands in furious notion. There's money involved in the case, and in any way she forbids the man from making such a claim.

"What deal?"

Rufus plays it hard to persuade and assures her of its authenticity.

"The chronicle had money to be shared amongst the beneficiaries of his partners. And the deal, it's the President," he clears his throat. "Don't pretend to be ignorant."

She glares at him, and buzz frowns outside; it's the chainsaw trimming a piece of wood by the keeper in the yard. She lurches toward Rufus with an impulsive anger.

"You're not getting the money, Rufus."

"Well, then I have to inform the police about your daughter."

He skips the conversation and ignores her. Rufus holds his briefcase and is about to turn toward the exit door. An alarming scream echoes; the old French man falls to the floor. Blood drips, emerging from his skull, as Rufus lies motionless. Slowly, the red pigments get outspread, marking a solid outline as it stains. *Is that a threat?* Leona Hill stands baffled over her deed. On her right, she holds the broken vase, and the rest of the pieces are smeared with the old man's blood. Rufus Young is dead.

The chainsaw-wielding keeper rushes in. His strength helps to transport the body to the coast. Quite far from the lighthouse, Rufus Young is buried as an unknown, unclaimed person.

When the sun goes down, the keeper makes love to Leona Hill in his attic.

CHAPTER SEVENTEEN

The School

Eighteen-year-old Daisy Collins stands in her blue jeans and white tank top. She feels the summer heat. On her right shoulder, she lugs her bag, containing some novels and history books for her new classes. She walks through the gate, unnoticed by others who seem indifferent to her presence. To her, it's the first day of attending school since her return to Brooklyn. She's nervous and anxious about everything she has gone through. Aching with it, she tries to keep a low profile and follows her path through the corridor toward her section. At noon, she is summoned by the director. She hesitates but can't avoid the call. She prepares herself, rehearsing her words, and answers with deep breaths and intense repetition. She steadies herself before knocking at the door. She shifts her thoughts, twitches along the corridor, and then shifts her bag to her left shoulder. She knocks at the door.

"Come in."

She hears the husky voice. Her spine shivers, and in a terrible conundrum, her feet advances. Quiet and submissive, she stands before the work desk. She observes how the director looks at her, seemingly frightful but tender.

"Good to see you, Daisy," says the school director.

She nods, saying nothing but listening to the authority. Then she inches herself forward and lay her fist on the support chair.

"I apologize for my cause."

"I've seen it in the media. Well, to be sure, you're safe here. You can attend school, and I assure you, no one will know about your presence," adds the director.

"Thank you."

"One question," the director inquires, "why did you do that?"

For a brief second, Daisy quivers in terror, petrified, and agitated in panic. She wasn't anticipating what the Director would ask, despite his earlier warning that he couldn't guarantee her complete safety.

Daisy fetches some thoughts from memory back lane and dispatches at face like she never did before. She seems aware of the consequences but that moment she needed someone who should know her side of the truth. Summoning her courage, she speaks bravely.

"I did it to protect my mother. To keep her away from a sinful man. He was treating her badly."

The director nods silently, his expression unreadable. She assures her again and ends the meeting. Daisy leaves quietly.

As she turns to leave, she stifles, stumbling over a query.

"Just to be sure, did you know the Statesman?"

Daisy nods certainly, "Yes, Mrs. Nora."

"Oh! Lord," she sighs.

Nora, the director, watches her exit the door.

In days, Daisy Collins gets acquainted with the ambience. She begins to feel the aura and her old self. She makes a new friend in her English class, and often passes the time with her until school is over. Weeks go by without her talking to her mother, nor does she yearn for it. The room appears the same as she left it. On her first weekend, she arranges it back to how it was. The television set is in the same spot, and the couch is slouched feet away, facing the screen. She prepares dinner for the evening, and her newly-made friend receives an invitation. Her intention is clear, to observe the bulletin and stay informed with updates. She waits for her company and glances at the clock. It ticks seven p.m. Out of curiosity, she calls her friend. A minute later, she hears a knock at the door. Daisy opens it, breathes, relaxes, and they embrace each other. She sets the couch and settles in well. The television entertains them with a comic show.

"What took you so long?" Daisy asks.

"It's the traffic jam, you know," says her friend.

Their time together increases as they rely on the longingness for one another. Daisy sets the dinner and they move to the spacious room where the couch gives them easy access to the TV screen. They put on their best show and linger in the happiest moments they can share. Her friend spends the night with her, and the next morning is a holiday. It's Sunday, and they decide to walk along the Brooklyn Bridge Park. The sunny day casts a spell by evening as vapors begin to rise from the East River. By dusk, they return, covering themselves from the torrential rain. Daisy drops her friend off on the way and she lingers outside for a while until she finds her way back to her room. Wet and slightly sluggish in her attire, she casually searches her closet for a new pair of night dress, and then sets off to prepare the dinner. She's cautious and alert about the day's happenings. Her customary routine remains the same with the television on, as she waits for the whistle to blow. The updates are known to her evenly at all times, allowing her to flick through channels of her choice.

The night, she makes a decision and calls the lighthouse keeper, rather than her mother. A conflict of unresolved hormones arises within her. She starts to hate Leona Hill more than ever, not because she dislikes her, but because of the cruel intentions revealed to her. Daisy converses with the keeper and inquires about her mother. A positive emotion surges within her, a notion she intended from the man. She feels relieved by the news and the longing desire to hear about her mother's whereabouts. As she watches the screen, the night overtakes her. The rain stops, but the gusting breeze enters through the window. She falls asleep on her couch, forgetting the rest of the world.

Time hasn't changed much, or so it seems. It's been a month since Daisy began attending her school. On the day the news surfaces, she walks across the street, pondering her test in the afternoon. She meets her friend on the way and decides to hurry as they are running short on time. Whispers are everywhere, soothsayers, and blabbers predominantly echo their silent voices in the air. Alarmed and startled by their presence, Daisy feels awkward as she walks through the premises. Eyes stare at her, the scary notion forbidding her from being the good girl, an unclear intention from all the watchers.

"Why is everybody acting peculiar today?" says her friend.

"Something's wrong," says Daisy.

They walk quickly and shut the door of their classroom, finding it empty. Daisy comprehends something is amiss and makes a call to the keeper.

"You're everywhere, Daisy," the keeper tells her.

She panics, trembling, her feet unsteady as she feels the perspiring trauma. She waits for no one and flees immediately. Her friend tries to provide comfort amidst the unknown commotion. Later, Daisy discovers the context of the incident that shook the city.

Daisy hurries back. On her way, she covers her face, protecting herself. Upon reaching her room, she turns on the television. She's everywhere again, but this time she finds it on an unalike context. The channel describes her as a fugitive who went missing. She sees herself on the screen, her picture framed in the corner, with a line seemingly provoking the search for her. The NYPD specializes in the hunt for her, and at any cost, she wants to keep a low profile, concealing herself from the rest of the world. She quivers on her feet and then falls onto the couch. A gentle mark reminds her of the face she sees on the screen. Susan Kelly talks to the correspondent of Fox news and shares the preliminary affairs.

Daisy waits, enveloping herself inside the room. She cages herself from the visibility of others, quarantining herself from the rest of the world. She doesn't want to be discovered by any known faces, or those hunting her. That night, she dials the keeper again, seeking assistance. She conveys her need for his presence. She hopes positive of the keeper and lately gets an assurance of his assistance. The keeper promises her to note his presence. Of all the escapes she has tried, locking herself in now seems the only option. She waits for a day or two for the keeper to appear at her door.

At the break of dawn on Wednesday morning, there is a hard knock on the door. The sound rumbles through the neighboring apartment. Daisy lies asleep, unaware, and unconcerned about the important odds. The door is hit harder, louder, and more uneven. This time, the noise draws attention. She opens her eyes steadily and places her feet on the cold floor. Her footfalls take a silent path as she marches toward the door. The knocking continues.

She clears her throat and wets her dry tongue. She shivers and her feet trembles.

"Who is it?" she asks.

Her voice fades at the door's end. The vibration lingers on. She pushes herself against the door, straining to hear from the other side.

"It's me, the keeper."

She hears correctly, recognizing the voice. Momentarily, she feels elated and opens the door. The keeper rushes in.

"What took you so long?" he asks.

"Unconscious."

"Are you on drugs?" the keeper inquires.

"No. Will you help me get out of this place?" she asks.

The keeper peers at her strangely. "Are you kidding? You have no idea about the spies behind these walls. They are everywhere."

"You can't leave me here forever. I don't want to go to prison."

"For now, it's best to stay hidden."

The keeper spends the night, helping her prepare dinner. As usual, the television speaks of the same concern. Daisy gets a bottle of wine, pours two glasses, and serves the man. He sits well versed, catching the context on the television. He lingers, deep and intense, as she takes a corner place on the couch. The keeper hears about the missing French man from the hotel Grande Albergo delle Palme. His dry throat goes off, grappling to resolve. He paces back and forth on the couch, sipping the wine and getting to his feet.

"Are you alright?" Daisy asks.

Daisy finds him impatient and distasteful in conduct. She walks up to him, urging him to calm down. His intense eyes glare with a desirous call. The keeper pulls her close by the waist and begins to kiss her. Wild, savage, the foreplay continues. He pulls off her tank top and presses himself against her breast, cupping them with his smooth palm and fondling them. Smoothly, he draws down her pants and shifts into position. He stands naked, watching her stripped figure. With emotive gestures, he begins to fuck her on the floor. Daisy moans wildly as the pleasure courses through her senses.

The television rumbles as the night proceeds, and their lovemaking continues.

In the fading twilight, Leona Hill stands in her front yard and watches the oceanfront. She finds no activity at the coast of the lighthouse. The roar of the waves reaches her as her silent call falls prey to some dubious play. She feels the absence of the keeper as darkness crawls in. The oceanfront remains dark for the rest of the night. She turns back, casting a narrow glance at the lighthouse, and walks inside.

CHAPTER EIGHTEEN

The Onslaught

The Hotel Grande Albergo delle Palme becomes the talk of the city. When press and correspondents thicken during the morning hour, Tony appears on the site. The entrance brims with crowds from different sects of agencies. The avenue has become the most popular spot in the last few months, and no place has gone empty without it being mentioned. Whether for its goodness or the worst, the hotel didn't miss its spot on every headline. Tony tussles amongst the mob and finds his way inside. He glances at the décor of the entrance whose flower-holders had gone missing. He hears from the horde somewhere in the swarm: *Seal this hotel, it's a bad omen to the city.* He turns back and forth to find the culprit, but in vain.

"Tony," calls one of the correspondents from NBC.

He waits for the man, being patient. "How can I help you?"

"What's your take on the case of the missing French man?"

"I do not want the negative reaction amongst the people, and I plead not to do so. We're working on it and very close to unwrapping it. Thank you."

Tony walks in, and the elevator lifts him to the fourth floor. Suite no. thirteen remains untouched since Rufus Young went missing. The examination begins with an intense exploration of the room. Tony walks toward the tea table and holds one of the cups that remains a print of the old French man. Then he strides toward the end of the window. The edges are wet, and the frames are worn out. The repair has not been done. He watches the children play in the garden.

"Who was the host to the man?" Tony's voice reverberates.

"It's Arthur, sire," replies one of the attendants.

"Send him in."

He keenly observes the artefacts from the medieval period representations. Then he gushes in toward the bathroom. He finds nothing wrong with it.

"What's wrong with this suite?"

Just then, the bellboy presents himself. Tony watches him, sharp at the corner of his sight. Something unusual he senses. Arthur shivers, and his feet are unsteady from the unknown commotion.

"Arthur, what did you do with the evidence? I can see some role of sabotaging play."

The bellboy breathes and stands in a frightful heart, lanky and slender with the uniform. He senses the fear; something went wrong with the old man who didn't return.

"I'm sorry, sire. I can't say I have a role. He only gave me a dollar bill for my service," says Arthur.

He takes out the dollar bill from his left pocket.

"He must have liked you."

"Indeed, we shared a common walk once in the garden."

"What did he mention?"

"Nothing, sir. He talked mostly about the French reverie and his pipe."

"The old man seems to be secretive," adds Tony.

Susan arrives and takes the old elevator to suite no. thirteen. Her footfall taps hard on the floor. She looks elegant and distinguished at the same time. Stands next to Tony and utters her favorite line of the day. *What's the junkie?*

"You seem to be not out of your hangover," chortles Tony.

"What's about the media and the press outside?"

"They won't leave alone. Troubling is their duty," adds Tony.

She watches him examine him and then concludes. His team walks forth through the door and takes the second elevator on the floor.

"There's something I need to tell."

"I'm supposing that."

"There's something unusual about the keeper in the lighthouse."

Tony halts and looks at her clearly to find something more serious. He nods his head and repels his face toward the staircase.

"Shall we take the staircase?" he insists.

"You aren't serious, right?"

"Well, I doubted the keeper a long time ago. It is not new. Tell me something about which I have no idea," says Tony.

They walk down the staircase. The lobby stands empty and unpersuasive to any guest attending the hotel event this evening.

"There's a grave adjacent to the lighthouse."

It pulls the attention of the man. Tony sets back and burns a cigarette as they walk out of the hotel. The horde still lingers, pertaining to questions. They avoid it and rush back to the headquarters.

Tony moves back and forth and leans on his desk.

"Do you mean to say it could be Rufus Young?"

"As of no evidence, it could be anyone, Daisy Collins or Rufus Young," adds Susan.

"That's a mess."

Susan waits for his final words. Perhaps her intention remains fine of wanting the keeper to be charged. Dig the grave and find the harrowing corpse.

"Aren't you going to do anything about this?"

"Collect evidence," says Tony.

She agrees and walks out of the chamber. She isn't pleased or persuaded by the approach. However, she lingers as per the suggestions behind the law. She appears frustrated and discontented with all she has done so far. Nothing profound has yielded yet, which makes the crisis even worse at this time of catastrophic circumstances. She waits for the sun to go down and watches the skyscrapers from her window. Then the setting sun dwells on the fading light that emerges from the horizon. She packs and rescues herself from the four walls. By sunset, she's seen at the bar. Massy Paul gives her the usual glass.

"What's wrong with the cop?"

"I'm glad you run a bar."

"What makes you say that?" says Massy.

"Just nothing," Susan sighs.

"Are you alright? Alan's here, you could share with him your unpleasant occasion."

"Is it Friday?"

Massy nods.

At dusk, Tony gets an informative detail. The onslaught has began. He drives toward Bronx, where a house of illegal activity lineage to Blanford Sky operates. It said those people belong to him and took over the business after his demise. Tony recklessly follows out with few of his men, armed with assault rifles and guns. The sources is right, it's at the club, an underground vault where they hide the narcotics. The club is used for supplying girls across United States arriving from different parts of the world. It's a hub for party, gatherings and entertainment.

The spot was filled with hordes and only adults were allowed inside. Sex, drugs, and alcohol are very much part of the social gathering. As the sun goes down, the music comes into play, while deep below at the vault, the business surges. The illegal immigrants have become experts in their doings and make cash from any source. Tony and his men arrive, disguised in their appearance, and make an entry, leaving behind a few to guard and protect outside. He loads his gun before entering, and he gets stopped at the door. The watchmen stop him along with his men and make a thorough inspection.

"Show me your ID card," in a Mexican accent.

Tony reaches into his pocket and picks out the fake name.

"Who are these men?" inquires another.

"They are my friends," says Tony.

"Hola," the rest greet.

The barricade allows them to get in. It's a massive foyer and every inches an individual gets rammed. The horde is real. The numbers are more as they crush deeper into the vault. The sources sign toward the direction, and as they slither in silent gestures one step at a time, Tony and his men get prepared with the ammunitions. He cracks the door, rams it hard and it shatters into two flaps. Then points at the men inside. He cracks his loud voice. *Surrender and put your hands up!* Tony and his men take immediate positions.

The gang was in a state of menace, bewilderment and confusion at the same time. None had any idea what was going on. From the outside, a voice creeps in; *it's the cops.* The assailant picks up a gun and starts to shoot. In retaliation, Tony's men fire back at them. The shootout continues for minutes, and the bloodshed follows on as the sound of the machine thrusts into the air. The scream rumbles on the floor, and the scattering of hordes randomizes the entire thing. People in the state escape from wherever they can. Tony sees that in minutes, the entire room gets loaded with dead bodies and blood spilling on the floor. The dead lay motionless, with bullet shells scattered around. He captures the living assailants and traverses back to the station. The inmates are sent to prison, and later they are questioned about the murder of Blanford Sky. It raises the question of the shootout at Broadway.

CHAPTER NINETEEN

The Secret Chronicle

Daisy stands in the dark room, the flickering light from the television casting a glint across her face. She deciphers the day she murdered the Statesman. While escaping, she held a scroll in her hand. On her instant note, she begins scavenging the entire room for the so called secret liners. She gets exhausted doing so, and on her last attempt, she gets the nudge of it underneath her closet, laying in dust on the floor. She stretches her arm to the end and uses her fingers to reach the paper scroll. She flattens herself on the floor and manages to get it out. Until that day, she remembered it and felt some significant stuff must have been jotted down. She sits and relaxes on the couch at the hour of midnight. The sound of the television mumbles as she opens the scroll on her desk. It said *the secret chronicle*, and below the headline was a long list of names. She browses through the words and then reaches the point of the President's assassination. She turns to the chronicle and finds more of it. The schema of the entire plot. And then the distribution of millions of dollars to the partners. She reads on her mind that *the Statesman was up assassinating the President for political power gain*, but the money hasn't gone to anyone yet. Also, the President isn't assassinated, a failed intention as it probes. She suggested to herself that she keep the chronicle safe and protected.

However, within the darkness of her four walls, she feels exhausted about being away from the rest of the world. It chokes her from hiding from the cops and leaving her in exile from human contact. Knowing the fact that she is in trouble, she can't afford to stay out of sight, for she needs the light to engulf her. Daisy feels skeptical about the chronicle to share. However with the narrowing of her choices, she finally decides to share the concealed Chronicle with the keeper, for she has some hope of assistance from the man.

Perhaps this could be one cause that her mother's attitude toward her has changed extensively. Leona Hill knows about the Chronicle. The late Statesman must have given a hint to her long time back. Daisy contemplates on the consequences. For that matter, Leona Hill doesn't want to get discovered by all that she knows about it. Daisy feels worst and laden with thoughts. The reason why their bond began to decay in the first place.

The morning glimmers as she observes through her window, the livelihood scatters and the passion of people walking through the streets. She laments as she watches them. Her memories regain, as her longing thoughts puts back her in the past. Unsettled, perturbed by her situation and circumstances, she decides to uncover herself. Daisy walks out of her apartment that early morning. She gets the idea to find refuge in an undisclosed location, a park known least amongst people. She enjoys the absence of other beings around as she grazes herself into a quiet ambience. She finds refuge in the novel that she held. The hour passes with no one to observe her. It gives her assurance of secure notion, as none are able to recognize the culprit. When the daylight eventually falls on her, she tries her best to escape the chaos. The noon lightens by the time she reaches her apartment. As usual, she puts on the bulletin.

She can't stop thinking about her mother. She's plagued by unsettling questions about why they drifted apart. It all happened because of Blanford Sky, she blames again and again. She is reminded of the days when she used to argue with her mother, but now she's at the juncture where she finds herself threatened by Leona Hill. Perhaps, she realizes, one day she might even assault her to death. Daisy remains cautious.

She waits for the dusk to engulf the edge of the day, and when the sun goes down, she enters her kitchen and prepares her meal. She feels the exhaustion and resentment crowding on her. She is so deeply saddened by her deeds that she laments over her past. She sheds tears at times, feeling vulnerable. Daisy lies on her back on her couch and catches a glimpse of her show on television. Her solitude reciprocates the way she begins to handle herself. At midnight, when the clock ticks twelve, she dials the number that makes her feel reliable – it's the lighthouse keeper.

"What's up?' says the voice from the other side.

"When are you coming to help me escape?" Daisy sounds tense.

"Soon."

"There's something I need to tell you. It's important."

"What's that?"

Daisy rises to her feet and walks toward the window. She lets the breeze in, and peers outside. The streets are empty and hollow in both directions. She scans back and forth below her apartment. In the distance, she glimpses the view of another ghetto area.

"There's a chronicle I found about the slain Statesman."

The keeper wakes up from his bed, takes his medication, and then reverts to the voice from the other side. He listens attentively and breaks his silence.

"What does it say?"

"You need to see it for yourself," responds Daisy.

An hour later, Daisy hears a thud, a knock at her door. She feels a sudden tremble running down her spine. She clears her throat and clenches her medium-sized fist. As she draws closer to the door, she senses the presence of someone – an elderly woman, coughing.

"Who is it?"

"I need the rent money."

The elderly woman coughs again. It's her landlady. Daisy relaxes and opens the door for her. Fortunately, she seems partially blind in her left eye. She enters and waits inside, her priority being addressed. She watches Daisy keenly as she scribbles to find the money from her closet desk. Daisy counts the bill and hands them over, waiting for her to leave. However, the departure isn't immediate. The landlady scans the room and notices the chronicle lying on the table, sparking her interest.

"What's that?"

Daisy swiftly hurries to fold the roll. "It's nothing. Just my school work."

She watches the landlady move out slowly. At the door, she stops and turns back to her.

"You look familiar. I've seen you somewhere."

"Yes, I live here. Now, you should get some rest."

Daisy slams the door shut and takes a deep breath.

"She's the girl from the television," the old woman mumbles as she walks upstairs.

Daisy feels weary. She thinks people now recognize her easily, in an odd manner. She's scared and suffering terribly from deep depression. Those legions aren't leaving her anytime soon. The chase is still on. However, amidst the chaos, she remembers her promise and the conviction she once held. She didn't want to end up in prison; her fight continues. Things have turned weird, uncanny now. Issues of trust gamble with her life, the relation she had shared with her mother has faded into oblivion. She no longer can rely on her nor expect the good out of it. Deep inside she's crying for help from wherever it arrived. But no one stands by her side. The mistake she made convinces her and encloses her in a tiny emotional cage of chaos and turmoil. In that darkness of life, she finds selfless love for herself, the rudimentary of all things she craves. Likewise, she keeps her inner spirit alive as long as she finds her path.

Daisy lay on her couch after the landlady leaves. Before she dials the keeper, she glances at the chronicle. Midnight seems the best time for her. She fantasizes about the love-making with the man and keeps him alive in her thoughts.

At the start of a new week, she gets an unexpected and uninvited visitor. It's her newly made friend from the English lessons. The morning claims its gloomy part, with slight drizzles cooling the day. Many neighbors mark their day on with the chaos of running to their workplace. Daisy hears multiple footsteps running and swarming down through the staircases of her apartment building. She's aware and conscious, although her eyes are shut and drowsy at the same time. Her couch provides her the best solution as an alternative for a sleeping place. She dreams of herself escaping Brooklyn just how she did in the past. It's a rare escape she validates.

At the door, the knock keeps coming, the footfalls keeps pouring. She hears none of it, again it's her speculation, the foreplay of vision running on her mind. The thud increases by itself. And then the voice reaches her ear, calling out her name from the outside. Daisy feels the tug of it and promptly stands on her feet with fear crawling inside her.

"Who's at the door?" she speaks loudly.

The friend responds from the other end. Daisy breathes and unlatches it.

"What are you doing here?" she adds.

"I was worried about you," her friend says, sounding concerned. An intent of care surfaces out of her.

"You shouldn't be here."

"I have seen the bulletin, you are everywhere. The cops are after you. I have also heard there's a bounty on you."

"What am I supposed to do?" sighs Daisy.

"Run, run from here."

"Do you think that's possible? I would have done it long time back. But, I'm everywhere; everyone knows me now."

"Did you really kill the Statesman?"

Daisy shakes her head assertively. She doesn't add anymore words to end the sentence. Then, she gets a glass of water from the kitchen.

"I'm sorry I can't assist you with this."

"You should go," she adds.

She watches her friend leave the space, then marches toward the window, looking below to see her friend go and the gloomy sky pretending to be clear. She feels a surge of bizarre, uncooperative feelings, and a strange defiance of compelling emotions within her. She submits to them.

CHAPTER TWENTY

The Woman in the Lighthouse

Leona Hill visits the keeper on a fresh morning, the day when her husband passed away years ago. She remembers it well. Henceforth, she feels the need to make the imprint of her memory more vivid. Her heart pounds deeper as she strolls over the gravel and sand along the coastal shore. She breathes as fresh as the ocean air gulfs her. Her intention remains calm, for she came in search of the keeper as well, noting how he went missing the earlier day. The empty lighthouse stands detached and is not known to people. She waits on the dunes for a while and watches the horizon. The gulls fly above and the sunshine emerges steadily. Gradually, the thin line of the horizon disappears from sight. Her feet stroll toward the lighthouse. The attic door is unfastened. She feels the warmth of sunshine falling on her. In a steady manner, she chases in the direction and pushes the door open. She makes it look like thievery so as to make the minimal amount of noise. The door creaks, unheard to the nearest, and her feet takes forward. She swallows a lump of saliva, and a slight escalation of fright renders itself upon her. As she draws closer, she trembles more. She finds the presence of the keeper from her point of view. Momentarily, she feels the existence of some guilt and ceases the series of steps. She waits silently and watches the keeper. The discomfort is seen in the action of the man. Back and forth, in an insane manner, the keeper tries to find something out of the trunk underneath the bed. Lately, the face has exposed its jovial nick after finding an injection needle. He fixes it on the desk, and the syringe is ready. The keeper inoculates and pulls a hormone from a small vial, which he instantly injects into his body. He seems to be in pain for a while as he lays his head down on the desk. His breath echoes in the large attic.

Leona Hill gets closer as she walks steadily toward the keeper.

"Tell me who are you?" her voice creaks.

The keeper lifts his head and stands on his feet. Turns back; his appearance raises a question, chilling, and daunting to handle. His eyes are raging in red, and his arms are stripping with nerves as he walks closer to her.

"Don't be afraid," he says.

Leona finds a difference in his tone. Then she forces herself to the table and finds the vial. She reads the label; it's a male hormone.

"What the hell? Tell me the truth! Who are you?" she raises her tone.

"I'm the keeper."

He seems malignant and draws one step at a time closer to her. Leona gets a hunch and pulls a knife from the table.

"I know who you are. You used to be a woman," says Leona. Her trembling hand points the knife at him.

"You caught me. I used to be, but I'm a man now."

"And you fucked me, you piece of shit. I'm going to go call the Sheriff."

Leona tries her finest effort to escape. She gets dragged down a series of steps before she is able to make her way out of the hollow attic. In the altercation, the keeper wins. He ties her with both hands and legs and sets her aside in the corner of the attic.

"You aren't going anywhere," he says.

He has the knife whizzing through her neck.

"Fuck you."

The keeper stands on his feet, displays a nasty smile at her, and walks off.

"See you in the evening. I've got some work to do."

She watches the keeper walk up and raises her voice.

"Have you been fucking my daughter?" she says in an annoying tone.

He doesn't respond, but an awful smile with a savage expression shoots out. He latches the attic door from the outside.

Fuck...fuck...fuck....Leona screams, on top of her voice, an array of angst and anger.

Long ago, before the arrival of the keeper, he used to be Isabella Cott. Raised by mixed-race foster parents, she ran away from the foster home. However, she later got discovered, and until the age of fifteen, her custody was placed at a children's rehabilitation center in Long Island. As a kid, her nature predicted her behavior, which seemed obscure and frightful at some point. Scarcely she had female friends then: she gazed at boys and cultivated their habits. She fashioned herself as a boy, conducting herself as a grown man would do. That astonished many in the rehab center. She has never allowed any boy to touch her.

Isabella Cott came out as a complete man by the time she became an adult and worked in many places, usually preferring male-dominated tasks, but because she was female, she got discarded. Later, for ten years, she worked as a maid. An issue she wanted to resolve was that she needed money. She wanted to be a man, and she loved it. She decided to change her sex and become the person she wanted to be.

Once, a local magazine covered her story of killing a young boy in the rehab center. For days, the chaos continued. The locals were in favor of ending the life of Isabella Cott. However, she got the protection of the county sheriff and later shifted to another undisclosed location. When she got out of the rehab center, her foster parents wanted her custody back, however, she denied the choice and wanted to make a living of her own by doing small jobs. On the day she was released from the rehab center she turned fifteen. As she waited for someone to take her away, she found the presence of her foster parents.

"I'm not going with them," said fifteen-year-old Isabella.

"They are your parents," said the matron.

"No, they adopted me. I didn't belong to them."

"That's your past. You can't be the same again."

"I want to be a boy," added Isabella.

The matron looked at her keenly but was perplexed by her varied impressions of the girl.

"Only if you go with them, you can become a boy," she added.

Then there appeared to be a smile on her face, and Isabella agreed to it.

A year later, she fled and never returned to her foster home. She did various jobs wherever she could, and by the time she turned into an adult, she could reason and make her choice. After working for ten years as a maid, she had gained some handsome money to fulfil her dream of becoming a man. She did turn herself into a man, a woman of familiar face who assists and supports her financially, on the note that no one could now recognise her old self. She feels proud of it and had lately forgotten about her rough past. She tells herself, she's no more an Isabella Cott but calls herself as Amos Cott. Isabella Cott goes for complicated surgical methods to change her sex, she amputes her breast from being a young woman into a broad-chested young man. In the next few years she continues her therapy, hormonal injections and thus the changes seem to appear. Her voice changes, her looks change, and beard starts to grow, a masculinity surfaces in her, and thus she renames herself Amos Cott, the lighthouse keeper.

Amos Cott recalls his tumultuous past, beginning with his birth in the suburban ghetto of Detroit, where he was rejected and ignored by his biological father. Escaping foster care, he endured the harsh streets, growing tough and resilient. In those days, he was a small girl child deprived of love and affection, surrounded by a diverse array of people with various habits, many of whom inflicted torment without reason. He witnessed drug abuse, homelessness leading to petty crimes like burglary and pickpocketing. Raised by a street couple who acted as his adoptive guardians, his adoptive father influenced him to follow a path of crime. One fateful night, chaos erupted when a police strike caught Amos's father in its trap, resulting in his fatal shooting. Amidst the ensuing turmoil, Amos and his adoptive mother, Isabella Cott, fled to New York, where they eked out a modest living through menial jobs. Isabella often asked about her father's return, only to be disillusioned when her mother revealed the truth: he was gone forever, taken by the police. As time passed, Isabella adapted to life in New York, forming bonds with other children in the neighborhood. However, tragedy struck again on a wintry morning when her mother was killed in a traffic accident, leaving Isabella devastated and orphaned.

Taken in by mixed-race foster parents, Isabella's experiences fostered deep-seated anger and mistrust towards others. Her angst and anxiety grew, shaping a rigid mentality that made it difficult for her to trust anyone. Meanwhile, Amos harbored a burning desire for revenge against humanity, viewing it as his sole purpose to eradicate those around him, particularly those who feigned kindness. This paradoxical behavior created a complex identity for Amos, oscillating between good and bad depending on his needs, yet always driven by his inner turmoil and desire for vengeance.

The final beam strikes the ocean surface as the light fades away into darkness. Leona Hill lay on the floor, breathing heavily. She hears the screech of a door. The keeper unlocks and strides down through the steps. He latches on before he comes down. He appears before her, bends on his knee, flexes and touches her hair. Then his hand runs through her body, breast and makes an attempt to kiss her. Leona tussles to escape the man but in vain: she shouts and screams. Her clothes are torn, her body bare, which enthused an intimate fondness. The keeper makes a strive and fucks her on the floor. Leona, helpless and defenceless, goes into a submissive state.

At night, he provides her dinner. Questions arise about the dubious tragedy.

"Why are you doing this?" Leona questions.

"For money."

"What money?"

"You will find it soon."

Leona looks at him keenly, then reverts to her plate. She doesn't eat the servings; instead, she asks for a cigarette, which the keeper fulfils.

"What's your real name?"

The keeper focuses on her and reckons from the chair. "Why do you bother?"

"Just curious."

He breathes and then sighs. "I used to be called Isabella Cott. Now I'm Amos."

"Isabella, what a beautiful name," adds Leona.

Amos pays her a last glimpse and prepares his bed. "You need to go to sleep now."

"Why didn't you like yourself?"

"Shut up, no more questions."

The keeper turns off the light. The attic goes dark.

When the attic door cracks three times, Leona wakes up on the floor. She whispers that there's someone. Amos wakes up, unsteady and drowsy.

"There's someone at the door," says Leona.

Amos straightens up and gets ready. He remembers about the deal the earlier day he fixed.

"I got it."

He prepares to walk up and takes a few of his shuffles.

"You could untie me. I'm not going anywhere. I know you're going to lock the door."

He breathes her out and then sets her free from the shackles. She watches him lock up as he walks out. Amos gets the demand he desires. He buys a shotgun from the man. The deal gets done in a quick cycle as he pays the man some money. Behind the attic door, Leona Hill watches through the slit, and as she tries harder, she finds it hard to get a glimpse of the man. She watches the seller drive the truck and walks off. Amos stands and bids a good deal with the man as he waits for him to drive away.

Leona tricks her mind and deploys an escape plan. She hides behind the door, at a corner of the hinge. She keeps watching for the return of the keeper. Her sharp gaze and keen sight keeps her alert. She hears the footfalls of Amos crashing closer. She waits for him to unlock and allows him to enter. The keeper sets in and trudges a few steps. As he does so, Leona jumps on him and dashes him down. He crashes below and falls hard, hitting the rocky floor.

Leona breathes harder as she strives to escape. She feels her legs burn and the gravel hurting her bare foot. Behind her, Amos follows, chasing. He stops at some point and aims his shotgun. He cries aloud, warning her. However, Leona pays no heed to the hint. She keeps her leg running. Her sight visions her house in the distance, the white picket fence calling her fast. *Cease or I shoot*, the voice clears the sky.

All at once, everything falls to silence. The sound resonates in the air and dies into the deep ocean. The scary gulls fly over the coast, and the smoke from the shot disappears into thin air. Everything slows down in a second. Leona Hill lay fallen on the sandy coast, blood dripping from her back, smearing across the ground. She breathes no more.

Amos Cott quickens to clear the ground and shovels the pit where he buried Rufus Young. He dumps her body and covers it again. For a while, he sits on the bump and lights a cigarette as he watches the oceanfront.

The day light inclines to the west when he walks inside the attic.

CHAPTER TWENTY ONE

The Story Behind the Scene

Susan Kelly listens to the song with her head down. She's exhausted, as her fatigue makes her feel heavy. She raises her head and sips the last remnants of her beer. The news bulletin keeps murmuring in the corner of the bar, lest she skip and pay no heed. Massy ruins her moment as she interrupts her with a smug. The cop doesn't answer. She keeps herself mum.

"Are you alright?"

Susan raises her head and pulls out the earpiece.

"Did you say something?"

Massy negates, being perky, and points toward the television. Susan turns her chair and leans back on the counter. She finds her friend resting her arms on the surface.

"Isn't she clever?" adds Massy Paul.

"What do you intend?"

"She knows how to escape."

Susan turns her chair, places her arm on the counter, and throws a coltish smile. "Will you get me another glass?"

Massy drops another glass for her and begins her usual conversation. "Why don't you take a leave and hang out with us? Just us."

"I would love to. I'm already exasperated by the stupid case."

"That's the reason why I didn't join the police."

She smiles and sips her beer. She feels the vibration of her phone. She glances at it. It's Tony.

"Now what the hell?" she purrs. She peeks at the time and receives the call. The noise disallows her, and she advances outside for clearance.

"What's up?"

"You should see this. You wouldn't believe," says Tony.

"I get that. Maybe tomorrow."

"Are you in the bar?"

"Sort of."

"There's a story behind the scene. You should come over," Tony persuades.

She drinks her remaining beer from the glass and hurries. "I will see you tomorrow," she says, galloping away.

"But what about the hang out plan?"

"Tomorrow," says Susan in her loud tone.

Tony waits for her at his desk. He reads the material on the computer screen. Then he shifts his chair, burns a cigarette, and looks out of the window pane. Manhattan radiates brightness from all sides, and then the honking below makes one wonder about the city. The multicultural effect makes it even more interesting for dreamers and artists around the world. He keeps gazing at the skyscrapers from his vantage point. As he decides to crawl back onto his desk, he hears the footfalls of Susan slithering in. She avoids the knock and walks straight forward to exhibit her presence.

"Don't tell me you found the culprit," she says.

Tony puffs his cigarette. "You shouldn't be surprised," he says, turning the monitor at her.

She observes with an insignificant gesture, "What's this?"

"These are the names of the registered lighthouse keepers of Long Island. And then there's something strange about this name," he points his finger.

"Amos Cott."

Then Tony displays the photograph on the screen. A familiar face emerges, which makes it look strange without any hint or clue, to be precise. Susan fixes her gaze keenly and deciphers it attentively.

"I know this keeper. He's the same person," she adds.

"How do you know?"

"I met him once at the lighthouse. He assisted us to find the house of Leona Hill."

"Did you find anything strange about him?"

She nods, remembering how close she came to this person. "Quite an unnatural conduct."

Tony surfaces the magazine on a new tab. Isabella Cott gets revealed. The article reads long as she interestingly puts her mind to knowing the story. Susan keeps her head still as she completes the last line.

"What do you intend from this?"

"Are you suggesting the keeper in the lighthouse was a girl?"

Tony breathes and takes his seat. "He could be anyone."

"Then who's this, Isabella Cott?"

"No idea, but this girl did kill a boy at the rehab center," adds Tony.

That night, Susan does some more research by herself. At midnight, she makes a call to Alan to get an information about their new errand. Then, before she goes to bed, she talks to her mother in Chicago. She learns more about the girl, Isabella Cott, and decides she will make a visit to the rehab center. She finds something strange about the girl, a deviant behavior, scarcely showing the traits of femininity but rather aggressiveness, as observations suggest. She comes to know about her foster parents as she browses more on the internet. It seems like a mess in the past, and hopefully, she believes both to be different people. Apparently, it suggests quite closely that they are the same person as she analyzes the rest of her learning about the girl. Certain traits reveal them to be same, but the absence of evidence makes it short to highlight the genuineness.

She falls asleep on her couch thinking about the girl. Somewhere in the corner of her heart, she still bears the pain of her heartbreak. The man she once fell in love with cheated on her in a very unconventional way. Since then, Susan didn't care to even make a contact with her former lover. She devotes herself to her duty to serve the city. When the time inclines apparently to the east, she's deeply involved in dreams, and the night welcomes them all, for the stories to be told aren't the same each night. She fixes it to share with her best friend in the bar, along with a glass of beer. At times, there's nothing for her to talk about dreams, a fantasy that she narrates as a tale, which makes her jovial momentarily. Massy insists she gets a date on many occasions, but she denies all attempts.

Susan drives to the headquarter when the clock ticks ten. She rings the rehab center. The voice sounds coarse, a female tone she expects. It's the matron. She makes an appointment, to meet and discover the details about Isabella Cott. At noon, she drives along with Alan toward Long Island. They land at the correct address and get a warm greeting from the matron. She allows them to get into her workplace, where a desk and chairs are arranged for the meeting. Susan scans around and peeps at the children outside in the playground.

"Please have a seat," says the matron.

Alan waits outside and watches the children play, taking part in their game as well.

"Tell me about Isabella Cott," Susan urges.

The matron draws a file out from the cupboard and hands it to her. She tells about her foster parents and then why she was brought in the rehab center. Susan's attention is drawn to the killing of the boy.

"Why did she kill the boy?" questions Susan.

"Isabella was a short-tempered child. Her traits never resembled those of a girl. Apparently, she had boys' company more."

"Do you know where she is now?"

"I handed her to her foster parents on the day she was leaving. I have no idea of her current whereabouts."

Susan breathes and nods her head in genuine notion. "There's a man in the lighthouse that goes by the same surname."

"I'm so sorry, I know nothing about the man nor heard of him."

"Fair enough. Thank you for your time."

Susan exits the work place and searches for Alan. They weren't over yet. When the sun inclines in the west, the shadows elongate, and they move out looking for the foster parents in the neighborhood. Susan stands steady before the door. Her fist knocks, and she waits silently. Alan hints at the absence of attendees. She knocks again; the response fails. They forge to walk back, turn around, and proceed toward the vehicle.

As Alan marks his footsteps, the door creaks and opens up. Susan turns around and finds a woman at the door.

"Yes, how can I help you?" the woman says.

"We want to know about Isabella Cott."

The woman calls them in and shares the background story. An hour later, Susan leaves Long Island and returns to the headquarters. In the evening, she gets the company of Alan and visits the bar. Massy Paul serves her the same routine and converses about their longing desire to hang out together. Under the radiance of multifaceted décor, Susan sips her glass of beer, keeps her ears open, and listens to her friend.

CHAPTER TWENTY TWO

Trap in the False Hand

It's the false hand that Daisy waits for. The long wait soon to come to an end. It's natural, she thinks, when one thing ends another begins. She lightens herself with her charming thought as she watches out through the window. As daylight ascends, the morning begins to warm up, children go to school, and the young and old move into the park. The ghetto surrounding appears in red from the walls of the houses on all corners. It's been a week, and the day has come, as she realizes it. She waits for the knock at the door. She will have to hurry and make the route to Long Island. A tough escape to go unnoticed, and then flee from vulnerability, she gathers her courage.

Her yearning comes true when she pays attention to the knock. She fixes herself and gets ready. She shuffles and opens the door for the keeper, Amos. The daylight sneaks in through the window. She shuts it up, an enclosure she shapes at the end of the room.

"We need to move fast," says the keeper.

Daisy Collins escalates her legs and swiftly moves off the streets to get in the car. Around the corner, a siren blows, the cops covering a patrol to gather information about the fugitive. Daisy keeps herself hidden in her hoodie and glides underneath the front seat. The keeper drives along, crosses few restraints from the cops, clears them easily, and flees out of the territory. Miles away from the city site, Daisy eventually sneaks out and uncovers her hoodie. She breathes and watches the coastal lines, the oceanfront gives her reminiscent call of her days that had gone by. She executes her mind to face her mother. She keeps herself mum and rests her hand on the window, feeling the breeze brushing her hair as they speed up.

"How's mother?"

"She's fine, but she told me to convey to you her absence from town."

Amos sounds as if he is making an honest confession. A false hope he displays for the girl. The game is a hoax, he knows well. She keeps silent again and waits for the smell of her yard.

"When did she will show up?" it strikes her again.

The keeper looks at her, steering the vehicle. "She didn't mention that."

The torturous lie.

Daisy expresses her gratitude to the keeper. She waits for him to drive toward the lighthouse. She watches as the sun goes down. She feels relief from her unsafe chaos. Finally, she breathes openly, and the absence of madness gives her peace. She walks in through the yard. Nothing has changed in her absence, and she pushes the door. Everything remains the same. She feels bad about her mother's absence, but at the same time, she feels elated that she's back home. She gets into the kitchen when the clock ticks nine, prepares dinner for herself, and watches the bulletin. Outside, the hollow sky roars in thunder and lightning. The wind blows ruthlessly, thrashing the window flaps. Daisy hurries to shut them all. The black cloud pours heavily. When she finishes, she rushes upstairs and fails to comprehend her mother's absence. A false notion engulfs her, with endurance she skips the night. Before she gets into bed, she pulls the window curtain away and calculates the rainfall. Her vision elongates, murky from her vantage point; the lighthouse is shining bright. Its beam stretches miles along the ocean line. Then she collects a novel, shifts to bed, and finds refuge in those words. The thunder and lightning guides her through the deep night until she falls asleep.

In the morning, she observes the keeper from her window. The cobblestones and the grasses in the front yard remain wet from the rain. She prepares cereal for herself and watches the bulletin. Her distress magnifies about her mother's absence, waiting and longing for her return. When the clock crosses half past ten, she strolls toward the coast in search of the keeper. From her vantage sight, in the distance, she finds him at the dock fixing his boat. The keeper is set to go for a long errand in the middle of the sea. He has nets and a fishing rod at the rear end of the boat. The keeper feels her presence and raises his head as he finds her walking through the dock.

"What brings you here?"

Daisy sighs, an expression of distress on her face. She blurts out her concerns about her mother's whereabouts.

"Did she say anything about her return?"

"To my knowledge, I remember none of that."

"I did make a call this morning, her phone rings but is unattainable."

"Don't you worry, she must have been busy. Do you want to come fishing?"

"No thanks, I'll stay at home."

The keeper gapes, releases the boat, and rows steadily as he distances himself from the anchor.

"See you later."

Daisy nods and waits for him to disappear in the far-off ocean water. She then sneaks around the place, heading toward the grave. She finds something strange about the hump, a sign of lofty grasses emerging from the ground. The cross has been removed, and barely anyone could recognize it underneath. Then her thoughts turn toward the hollow attic. She lumbers toward the dark hollow dungeon. She finds the unlatched door. Her feet drag her inside, one step at a time, and her breathe freezes for a while. The dampness makes it unstable, but she steadily makes her way down. She gets the smell airing inside the attic. It's pungent and toxic to inhale. She presses the switch bulb and makes it glow. The mess is inconsiderate, and she examines what went wrong. She scans all she can and finds no hint of any wrongdoing. Lately, her glimpse notices the table. There's something wrong, she figures. She gets closer to inspect. There's a syringe and a small vial in a first aid kit. She reads the label, as close as she can to not miss any words. It amazes her distinctly without any second thought. She trembles and stands in fearful affliction. The dismay numbs her for a while, then she reverts the vial back into the kit.

In the corner of the table, she finds a photo album. She flips it open and browses through a few of the pages, discovering the unnerving truth about the keeper. It's his childhood pictures as a girl, Isabella Cott. She runs out of the attic immediately and flees to her safe haven. All her way, she keeps thinking about the keeper in fear, realizing he's a woman, a transsexual evil, she remarks. The entire evening, she deciphers the truth about the keeper, his past, and the sex she committed. She feels guilty and curses herself for not unmasking the truth sooner. She experiences a setback and feels discomfort in her life. The lie about her missing mother depicts the suspicious nature of the keeper. She keeps it in mind to pursue the truth about the man. Hesitantly, she prepares dinner for herself and watches the bulletin, but she avoids it, as the odd has come into her life without warning. She plans to unearth the man, nervous and worried on many levels. She can feel the edge of her trauma affecting her body. Walking back and forth in the living room, floundering wildly in a confused state, she feels the tempest arriving from the distance, and a knock cracks at her door. She sets back, breathing heavily, and slowly takes her first step toward the destination. Her footfalls are silent and creepy at the same time. She hears nothing, and her skin is pale. Shivering down her spine, she pushes her ears against the door. She cranes her neck to find out, the knock is from the adjacent window. She can see the trousers of the man; it's the keeper. Her dry throat demands silence. She raises her hand and unlocks the fear. Amos slithers in as if nothing has happened. He makes a shallow smile and then proceeds inside, portraying a cocky demeanor.

Dusk has fallen, and the west reminds her of the day's end. Unfortunate as it is, she leaves the chronicle open on the table. Amos notices it. He picks it up and finds the schema of the truth. He breaks into a cruel laugh, money and the assassination of the President. Meanwhile, Daisy watches, waiting for the right moment to confront him.

"Tell me where's mom?"

Amos turns his face and rolls the chronicle. "Like I said, she's out of town on business."

"You're lying."

His intent remains uncertain and conceited as he moves toward her.

"I ain't lying, darling."

"Don't call me that. Reveal who you are!"

Daisy points a knife at him, standing steady and courageous. Her voice gets sharp and loud as she repeats her demand about her mother. She sees the man closing in on her. She waves the knife in the air, keeping him at bay.

"Calm down," says Amos.

He tries to pursue her, enforcing himself with cruel intentions. Somehow, the keeper reaches her and manages to break free the knife. An altercation ensues, a battle of strength, as he tries to force himself on her. Daisy gathers her strength and escapes the man. She sprints outside, pacing as fast as she can toward the main road. She senses the keeper pursuing her. She races faster, but her feet fails her. Her breath shortens and she slows down. Amos quickly catches up and grabs her by head, pulling and sweeping her onto the ground. He keeps her captive in the attic.

"I know who you are. You're a transgender."

Amos laughs, barbaric and savage. "So you did find out."

"What have you done to my mother? Did you kill her?"

Wild and brutish, "She was delicious" the keeper says, laughing.

CHAPTER TWENTY THREE

The Lineage of All

For detective Susan Kelly, her preference remains the same – she opts for accurate navigation of the conundrum. Her chaotic mind suggests she navigate the lineage of all those linked to the murder of the erstwhile Statesman and the French visitor Rufus Young. Over a week, she tries to unravel the interrelations of the conundrum that's been troubling her. Failing to find the fissures, she proceeds with her assignment. Isabella Cott and Amos Cott remain a mystery in the eyes of the beholder, as nothing surfaces nor are any clues exposed. The rumors are unsettling for Susan.

When the sun begins to set in the west, she takes some time to walk along the sidewalk. In a rush, she adores the crowd. Her cynical mind suggests her to look everywhere, but at the root, she grasps the order of her missing case – the incorrect lineage of the keeper at the lighthouse.

"What if both are the same person?" It strikes her hard as she waits for her burger at the outlet. She races back to her squad monitor. Her perky brain imagines the prospect that she thinks will yield her the way out. She types a list of surgery clinics that carry out transsexual operations. The Island reflects some of the reputed surgeons in the field, and she marks them all. She can't wait to procrastinate and emerges from her room with extravagant confidence. She makes a call to Alan before she heads out on her errand. She picks him up on the way and speeds toward the coastal road.

"Hope it's not a waste."

"Trust me, you're getting therapy after this," blurts Susan.

Alan laughs, quirky and sober. She halts and reads the hoarding. "That's it."

Alan follows, unaware of what's going on. He simply follows her commands and does as she suggests. Susan knocks on the door and gets an immediate appointment with the surgeon. The attempt fails to yield results. This continues for sixteen times, making Alan impatient and exhaustive.

"What are we looking for?"

"Wait, hold on. The show is about to begin."

On their seventeenth attempt, Susan finds the right clinic. She meets the doctor and explains the situation. She reveals the face of the keeper, but the surgeon doesn't recognize the keeper's face.

"Do you know anyone named Isabella Cott?"

The surgeon lingers on the thought and recalls a fragmented part of his memory. "Let me check the files."

"Who's this Isabella Cott?" Alan blurts.

"Yes. Isabella Cott. She underwent surgeries. She wanted to become a man. I did help her with that."

"Do you have any idea where she must be now?"

"She said she would be working as a lighthouse keeper, with a name change to Amos Cott."

"How do you know all of these?" Susan inquires.

"She mentioned it on the last day of her therapy session. She seemed happy."

"Seems like she must have trusted you a lot. Thank you, doctor, for your time."

"Has he done something unlawful?"

Susan sighs. "Doctor, you have done a good job."

The surgeon lingers on, perplexed and baffled at the same time.

Alan stands bemused and makes an incomprehensible discovery about what he learned.

"Are you saying Isabella Cott is the keeper?"

"Yes, Alan, but it seems she's no longer Isabella but Amos Cott."

They drive back with the gist of the information and the set of evidences. She drops Alan back at his place, asking him to come in the next morning. Then she speeds to the headquarters. She knocks on Tony's door, ignoring the rest of the formalities.

"I was right."

"Right about what?" asks Tony.

"They are the same person. Isabella Cott is Amos Cott. He's a transsexual."

"What's the source of evidence?"

She exhibits the doctor's file and hands it to him. Tony peruses the files, and the truth is revealed.

"You shouldn't waste any more time after this man."

Susan nods. "Quite a hard chase."

"The Mayor is in the city. He's here for an address."

"Right."

As daylight turns from yellow to orange and the shadows lengthen, the horde appears along the street side. The Mayor begins his address. The swarm of people cheers for their leader, and an uproar ensues as he speaks his first word. Susan stands beside her boss, watching the ceremony. The dusk falls, and the streetlights emerge from all directions.

"Fan of the orator," says Tony.

He observes the crowd and folds his hand.

"Portrays to be a good Mayor," Susan adds.

The Mayor announces the reopening of a theatre on Broadway with a new show. The showgoers applaud the decision and express their delight with the lawmaker. An hour later, the horde breaks apart, drifting and scattering as the Mayor leaves the spot. Susan wastes no time and drives to the bar where Massy prepares her beer glass. She sits in her usual spot at the counter and sips her beer.

"So, what's the plan then?"

Massy turns her head from the brewer machine and pays attention to the words. She follows with a jug of beer and pours in into the glass for both.

"I was wondering if we could go to Central Park this weekend."

"What's special about it? There are always a lot of people."

"Where do you want to go?"

"Some silence and peace would be nice."

"I got it. That sounds like a recipe," adds Massy.

Susan spends another hour in the bar. She makes a call to her mother and listens to the old woman's complaints, while Massy gets back to the brewer machine and fills glasses of beer for the newcomers.

Darkness crawls in, and the havoc is real. The wreck at the hotel Grande Albergo delle Palme creates a fuss amongst the crowd. The damage has been done; few lay dead on the roadside, and visitors remain hostage in the foyer. The masked man points his gun at everybody, demanding in a loud voice the presence of the executive. Tony gets the alert of the 911 call. He rushes with his few competent men to the spot. Hotel Grande Albergo delle Palme turns into a mess, a battleground. The masked man fires his gun from the foyer. The area is vacated immediately. Tony's men take immediate position to counter the onslaught. The rounds continue for minutes. The entrance fills with bubbles of smoke. The pots in the décor crash and demolish, and the debris scatters around. It's no longer a better place. One of the fine men makes to sneak into the foyer. There's only one masked man. The equipped cop fires at him unnoticed. The headshot makes the masked man fall to the ground instantly. Outside, the crowd gathers, the siren wails, the ambulance arrives, and the smoke rises in the dark air. The press waits for its story to be delivered.

Tony unmasks the man. "A villain," he says. Then, bending on his knee, he searches the pockets and gathers evidence. It's the chronicle. The man had a copy of the written chronicle. He reads minutely the conspiracy of the chronicle, *the money and the assassination of the President*, the failed attempt. Unaware of the fact of the missing French man Rufus Young, the masked man's errand was cut short in trying to find the old man. It's an unknown reason.

Tony heads out of the foyer with the chronicle in his hand. Reporters from various channels surround him. The questions pour in and he hesitates at first, then makes it sound diplomatic.

The headline falls instantly on several newscasts. Times Square displays a new headline that says, "The assassination schema of US President caught at Hotel Grande Albergo delle Palme." It flashes several times on the electronic screen. The mob reads it as they pass by. The print media makes it a terrific headline the next day.

Susan Kelly stands on her legs. She's supposed to be home. She bids farewell to her friend and walks out of the bar. At Times Square, she makes a halt, reads the bulletin board, unaware of the recent happenings at the hotel. She breathes and then drives her car.

CHAPTER TWENTY FOUR

The Last Dead Girl

Amos Cott thinks about it many times, remembering the horrific incident. He didn't want it to happen that way, but fate had something else in store for him.

When the sun began to set in the west, he returns from the sea. He looks up at the sky, watching the gulls return home from the far-stretching bay. He seems delighted and joyous. He fixes the boat and anchors it at the dock. In his right hand, he holds a big salmon; in the left, a harpoon; and on his back he carries the heavy fishing net. From the distant horizon far off the ocean, thunder and lightning calls down. It will rain tonight, he thinks. He reaches the door and fetches the key from his pocket. He stinks of a pungent odor, his clothes are torn, and his face looks quite scary. He stares at Daisy as he proceeds the steps. He drops his belongings on the floor and gets handy with her. He takes her hair and smells it, then tries to kiss her. She struggles, repelled, and pushes him with her strong leg. Amos falls off. His ego gets in the way, and he smacks her on the face. Daisy falls to the floor, hitting her head. He spits on her and shuffles toward the desk, saying, "You bitch."

Amos unpacks a syringe and fetches a vial of male hormone to inject. Daisy watches him in fear, silent and still.

“What did you do to my mother?”

He turns his back, a wild laugh following, scary and intimidating. The keeper behaves like a menace. He comes closer and bends on his knee.

“I fucked and buried her.”

She turns ferocious and screams at him, "Why?"

“I hated that woman.”

“You used to be a woman,” says Daisy Collins.

“I hated being a woman. They are the most fearful and inept creatures on earth, and so was your mother.”

Daisy fell on her knees, weeping and helpless. She yearns for melancholic remedy, gasping, and calming.

She recalls the good days spent with her mother, memories of wintry mornings when she ran to her father to bring fish from the sea to her mother. Suddenly, she begins to notice her absence keenly, despite their past conflicts. Somewhere in the corner of her heart, Daisy holds a profound affection for Leona Hill, the woman she once called Mother. She feels the void instantly, finding it hard and overwhelming in the circumstances. Amidst all these, she gathers her strength remembering her mother’s exact words: “Do not bow when a man overpowers you; weakness resides in us all, none of us are invincible.” These were the words she spoke when she wanted to escape from Blanford Sky. If she could defy the Statesman, then repeating the same wouldn’t be hard. Daisy articulates her vengeance against the keeper clearly.

“You don’t deserve to live,” Daisy sounds ferocious.

“And yet here I’m.”

“You’re weak and coward. You’re a shame to your kind.”

The keeper seizes her neck, gripping tight, his face exhibiting resentment, as Daisy struggles to breathe. "You'll have the same end as your mother."

She falls on the ground instantly on setting free, stressing out to breathe and warns the keeper, "Count your days, Amos."

Amos Cott exits from the attic looking frustrated and angry, dipped in agony, forging wicked intentions. Although Daisy seems to be optimistic about her notion, she feels her weakness lingering and depriving her of strength to revenge her mother. She's fragile and sickly exhausted. An hour later, the keeper provides her with dinner. She avoids it and lays on the floor.

Out on the ground, thunder and lightning strikes the surface. The storm arrives with a hungry blow, and the pouring rain trashes whatever comes in between. Wild and ugly, the night turns out to be. An invincible storm rules the night. The waves hit hard along the coastline, penetrating deeper into the sandy surface. The dunes are carried away into the ocean and pebbles are washed far off. At midnight, when the keeper falls asleep, Daisy raises her head from the ground, keeping an eye on him. She breaks free from the bindings and marches toward the door. She can't keep it quiet, it creaks. The wild storm doesn't support her. She paces outside through the ugly chaos. The wooden door bangs against the frame loudly, waking the keeper. He jolts awake and finds her missing. He picks up the shotgun and follows her out. He chases and shouts at her. His screams are diminished by the wild storm. Daisy, wet and heavy with her clothes, struggles to move forward as the wind pushes her back.

Amos can't hold back any longer and shoots her in the leg. Momentarily, she feels the pain catch in her brain and falls to the ground. She gets drenched in the rain. The keeper brings her back to the attic. Exasperated, Amos behaves rudely. He sees her drenched clothes and her body shaping beneath them, her cleavage exposed in a desirable fashion. "You bitch…you will never run away again," he repeated. He rapes her on the cold floor.

In the morning, when the storm is gone and the keeper is absent, Daisy tries to escape. She feels the pain in her leg. The door is locked from the outside. She worries and finds a way out from the attic. The chainsaw underneath the bed comes into her hand. She runs it and hollows out the wooden door. She fixes her mind, gathers strength and courage, and moves with her injured leg.

In the water, the keeper gets ready for his day's errand. He looks out into the far-off ocean, and fetches his harpoon and net from the dock. He sails for a minute into the deep. And unfortunately, the keeper sees the girl escaping quickly. He sails back to the dock as fast as he can. Amos picks up the shotgun and begins the chase. He stretches his voice, but Daisy is firm in her conviction to flee at her best. He takes a firm stance and aims at her. He pulls the trigger, and the noise resonates around. Lifeless, Daisy falls to the ground, her head smashed and blood dripping from the skull. The keeper hurries to the spot. He seems regretful, resenting his deed. He sits on his knees, an expression of guilt and misery sustaining on him. "Shit…shit…," he blurts.

He does the same thing later. He buries her in the same graveyard. The sun slants by then, and he watches it from the corner of his eye as he feels fatigue after covering the dead bodies.

"This is the last dead girl," he contemplates. He senses the guilt he has committed so far. His intention had failed him, for he didn't want her to die. He rests on the grave and fetches a cigarette from his left pocket. He inhales for a few times and watches the setting sun.

When the sun goes down, he picks up the shovel and his fishing instruments from the dock and encloses himself in his attic. He injects the hormone again. Laying overhead, looking up at the ceiling, he ponders over the past. He feels his heartbeat, the crusade coming. He dreams of fearful exploitation, the woman he once was. He wakes up screaming, "I'm not Isabella Cott!" His trembling hand searches for the syringe and injects more of the hormone. He sweats in his nervousness, for the world seems to be closing in, unveiling the truth to him. He swallows a pill and gets on his feet.

At the corner of the oval attic, he finds a lantern, illuminates it, and moves outside toward the stone wall house. He sees the white picket fence in haze and drags himself inside the house. He advances upstairs and looks in Daisy's room. He searches for some money and eventually finds some in the desk drawers, then trudges down. In the kitchen, he looks for some food. The refrigerator contains some wine and bread. He consumes them and watches the television for a while. The bulletin surfaces about the hotel Grande Albergo delle Palme. Amos gulps the pieces of bread and leisurely sprawls himself on the couch with his ears open. Despite the chaos, he seems relaxed and calm. After wasting an hour, he decides to get back to the attic.

On his way, he hears the wailing of a car. It's the Sheriff of the town. He stands with his lantern burning and waits for him. The car stops, and the Sheriff gets out of the wailing vehicle.

"Sheriff, what's wrong?" the keeper says.

"Where are you going?"

"I was returning to my attic."

The Sheriff briefly scans the area with his sharp sight. The darkness makes it hard.

"What's with the lantern?"

"Oh! It's because of the darkness."

The Sheriff nods. "I heard a gunshot."

The keeper acts natural and reluctant, pretending to be unaware of it.

"I'm not sure I'm quite aware of it."

"Just stay safe. You never know who might kill you first," the Sheriff warns.

He looks at him severely and then trudges back to the wailing car. Amos waits for him to leave. But he mentions his unavailability for a week. He gets close to the car, lantern burning bright, and conveys his message. He assures the Sheriff he won't be at the lighthouse for a week. The keeper will be gone to Maine to meet his grandmother, he insures.

"Alright, just a week."

"Thanks Sheriff" he says.

He watches him turn the car and drive away. In the darkness, he walks with his lantern and returns to his attic.

CHAPTER TWENTY FIVE

Corpses in the Lighthouse

"Will you explain what went wrong yesterday? I assume something wrong has happened," Susan enters, blabbering. She stands fixed in her stance and watches Tony sip his cup of tea, a customary morning practice.

"At hotel Grande Albergo delle Palme."

"Again, a shootout?"

Tony nods and pours tea for her. Susan takes a seat and flips through the newspaper. She reads the bulletin and sighs in despair. She sees the chronicle on the desk.

"What's that?"

"It's a chronicle. The conspiracy plan to assassinate the President."

"Are you kidding me?"

"Have a look for yourself."

She reads it meticulously and sips her tea. "There's a lot of money involved."

"The victim seems to be the direct benefactor of Blanford Sky. Look at the signature below, it's the erstwhile Statesman," replied Tony.

"Well, it's an adequate evidence to present before the court," adds Susan.

"What's your plan of execution today?"

Susan lands her cup on the desk and breathes in, folding the chronicle and leaving on the table. "I'm on the hunt to find the keeper."

"Good luck with that."

At noon, with few of her men, she moves out to Long Island. On the way, she picks up Alan.

"I can't believe the keeper was a woman."

"Neither can I, Alan."

She steers the wheel, quickening on the road. She accelerates along the coastal drive, past rows of houses. She perceives the lighthouse in the distance. Susan Kelly applies the brake and halts before the white picket fence. The stone wall along the side stands wet and dismantled. She senses an impulse of misdeeds, like something wrong has taken place. She barges into the house of Leona Hill, demanding her presence, but gets no response. She moves upstairs to Daisy Collins' room. She finds an unsettling closet in the desk drawer. Her strong intuition suggests her mishap. The chaos must have taken place quite a few days ago, she assumes, as she scans deeper. She dawdles along the window and lingers, her vision stretching toward the ocean-front. She elongates her sight and finds the distant lighthouse. The dock is void of the keeper. A few novels lay on the bed untouched, including the one with a bookmark, which Daisy might have been reading. She strolls down, moves toward the kitchen. There's a missing wine bottle and bread from the refrigerator.

Alan notices the untidy couch.

"I sense an intruder," he says.

"It suggests so," adds Susan.

They linger inside the house for another few minutes.

Through her vision, Susan observes the lighthouse from the door. She stares, sensing an evil presence. Then she opts to walk toward the coast.

"There's something wrong here."

Emptiness prevails, serene in nature, and the breeze rushes through them as they feel the dunes beneath their feet. They walk with their men and keep an eye on the premise. Alan inspects the dock, finds an anchored boat. The harpoon and the fishing net lay on the deck.

Susan cautiously holds the gun and opens the door to the attic. She's followed by two of her guards. Her heartbeat races as she prepares herself for any sort of counter from the opposite direction. One step at a time, she gets down. The attic is dark and empty, and their footfalls resonate. One of the guards light the bulb. It appears hollow, except a desk and a bed remain behind. The scrutiny begins. Susan walks around the attic and looks up at the ceiling. Then the dust makes it difficult to observe. At one corner, she finds the lens and equipment for the lamp atop. When she dashes against the desk, a small vial falls on the ground. She reads the label meticulously. It's a male hormone. She keeps it in mind and sorts it as evidence. Then there are ropes and some blood marks on the hard ground.

"There must have been a captive," says one of the guards.

Susan scans minutely and contemplates an imaginary scene. In her mind, she has already begun recreating the crime. She assumes it to be Daisy Collins's blood, an intuitive command.

"It seems the keeper has fled."

Susan trudges out of the hollow attic. Alan finds the harpoon and the fishing net and rod.

"There's a pretty boat out there anchored in the dock."

"I thought that. Amos Cott or Isabella Cott seems to be missing."

Her suspicious character reflects heavily on the deciphering ability that she possesses. She turns and glares sternly toward the site. The grave seems to disappear. There're no lumps of sand or the cross fixed on the ground.

"Get a shovel," she says.

"Now what?" Alan questions.

"There's something I need to show you all, guys."

The lighthouse tower stands tall in a huge column as they harrow the grave. Reaching a certain depth, they excavate three dead bodies, rotten and decomposed. Daisy Collins lifeless body seems to be recent, but much of it still seems fresh. Susan is taken aback. Her soul moves, her feet drifting from the spot, quite catastrophic, as it seems. She makes an instant call to the nearby health facility. The siren wails, and the ambulance arrives. In a moment, the locals gather around. The scene creates chaos in the town. The press and the media get the clue and arrive with their questions.

Meanwhile, Susan claims it to be barbaric, a savage act. The sun goes down, and darkness begins to triumph. In the chaos, she makes her way out of the spot. The area is seized. Tapes bordering from all corners set the perimeter. Camera flashes from all around, and the journalists begin exaggerating about the situation. They define their own headlines and showcase what the people fall for.

"Aren't you going to stop the media?" asks Alan.

"That's none of my business," replies Susan.

The dead corpses are put into the CPE bag and transported to the nearby medical facility.

"Who are the other two corpses?"

"I don't assume it to be, but I'm quite sure it's Leona Hill and the French old man, Rufus Young."

On the road away from the chaos, a siren car wails. It's the town's Sheriff. He finds the calamity around the corner and drives toward the coast. He looks oblivious and unaware.

"The Sheriff is here," Alan mutters.

She walks forward and waits for his presence.

"What's wrong, officer?"

"Well, you got to seal the lighthouse."

"What's the matter?" the Sheriff seems curious.

"We found three corpses under your jurisdiction," adds Alan.

"That's impractical."

Susan seems to be discontent. She holds grievances. "Do you know anything about the keeper?"

"I met him quite a few times. He said he would be going to meet his grandmother."

"And that's where?" Alan intrudes.

"Maine."

"Do you know he's a transsexual? He used to be a girl, a woman, Isabella Cott," Susan declares intensely.

The Sheriff stands numb, unable to comprehend the truth.

"He's a murderer," says Alan.

An hour later, Susan and her team retreat to the city. The bulletin makes another row of headlines that establish the failure of the State Police Department. Tony defies all that goes against them, whilst Susan makes it seem unbearable.

"Why do they always overemphasize?" blurts Tony.

"Believe me, the scene was horrendous," Susan mutters.

A long yawning gulf of silence prevails, as both retain to watch the television broadcast.

CHAPTER TWENTY SIX

The Reappearance

On Sunday morning, Massy Paul meets Susan at her residence. She finds herself preparing a toast and a cup of coffee. She offers a cup and takes a seat in the lavish apartment.

"I love the décor," says Massy.

She browses through the wall paintings and then shuffles toward the balcony. Massy appreciates the view of the skyscrapers and then remarks on the rising sun from the east. She watches Susan get ready with her attire.

"Let's go."

They were supposed to drive to New Jersey, where Massy's mother lived. Susan avoids her car; instead, she admires the Range Rover of Massy and agrees to it. They drive through the well-built freeway. An hour later, they halt at the drive-through to pack their lunch.

"I'm quite excited to meet your mother."

"She would be happy to see you," adds Massy.

In New Jersey, they get a warm welcome. Spend the entire day and share dinner before their return to Manhattan. It's a long drive again, and Susan takes charge of the steering wheel. She allows the air to slither inside and keeps her eyes sharply focused on the road. It's silent and quiet from both; Massy seems to be tired, and resting seems to be a necessary option.

The phone vibrates. Susan glimpses the name and slows down. She clinches onto her earpiece and utters her words.

"It's the Sheriff. There's some important clue I thought would be useful to you."

"And what's that?"

He orates, "I've seen the keeper with a woman quite a few times, just a few weeks ago."

"And who do you think that woman could be?"

"I assume it's her grandmother."

"That's not possible at all. Thanks for your insight," says Susan and hangs up the call.

The newly born dawn flourishes with the pouring of drizzles. The city is still in silence, and with seconds of crossing over, the droplets of water slow down. From the east, a warm glow rises on the horizon. The dawn breaks into a shining streak. Its first beam enters the rectangular space and falls on Susan's face. Her sleep takes off, and she feels the warmth of the day. As usual, she picks her morning routine, gets ready, edits, and devises her plan for the day. She sips her morning coffee and makes a short call to her mother before she drives.

She can hear Tony's voice as she walks through the aisle to her cabin. She doesn't waste time, gathers the papers, and follows inside.

"I've seen the report this morning. The NBC says it's a catastrophic crime."

"What about the New York Times? What did they print?"

"Look at it for yourself," Tony said, tossing it on the desk.

Susan takes a seat and denies the tea. She reads the headline – *A transsexual man guarding the lighthouse is suspected to be a common murderer.*

"How did they know about that?"

"They have been following us since the beginning," adds Susan.

She sees herself on the front page of the bulletin paper.

"You look great," Tony compliments the capture.

"There's something important I need to say. The Sheriff called me the other night and said he saw the keeper with a woman a few weeks ago."

"A woman, who could be her?"

"Says his grandmother."

Tony picks up on his feet, wades himself toward the window, and gazes at the distant horizon in the blank space. He turns on his heels and ponders the recent report. He hands the autopsy report to her. *She can't be Leona Hill or Daisy Collins at the same time.*

"Julian Baker has been missing from the city."

She gets a hunch about it. "Do you think it could be her?"

"Anything could be possible. All are suspects. Where does the grandmother belong?"

"Maine."

Susan Kelly intends to visit Maine in search of the grandmother. She picks up Alan and a few of her guards and drives the Chevy. She moves out quickly from the city and gets onto the freeway. Halfway through the ride, a biker follows behind. Susan plays it calm and pays no heed, as it seems quite another rider speeding up to catch the rest ahead. She maintains a close look through the rear mirror.

"I remember a week ago, Julian Baker showed up to me."

"What?"

It explodes as a shock to her. She steers the wheel, then looks in the mirror. The biker goes missing behind them.

"Where's the biker? Where's the biker?"

Susan gets terror-stricken and speeds up. "There's a biker following us."

Alan cranes his neck outside of the window and stretches to look back. The biker is right behind them on the opposite side. He gets the shotgun out and prepares to pull the trigger.

"Turn around. It's the biker."

Alan's voice pitches high. The shot fires. It hits the tires, and the Chevy cripples, tumbling on the freeway and crashing aside. The biker fires again. It hits Susan on her right arm, and she starts to bleed in pain. The guard fails to chase and opens fire at the shooter, but in vain. It vanishes in thin air. The keeper disappears, but no one potentially recognizes with the head cover. A sign of warning, the message he proffered.

The crash site evaporates in smoke. The locals gather and assist. Many seem to know the faces. Susan has become the most popular cop in the States by now. She's sort of a minor celebrity officer. Some talk about her appearance on television and applause rises from the local crowd. She waits for the medic, and the press comes clear, broadcasting the accident. While Tony watches the bulletin, a brief and urgent call is dialed.

Susan lies on the stretcher as the medic helps her into the van. She feels the vibration of her phone. The name flashes. She reaches it with her left hand and sounds in a shallow tone.

"Are you alright?"

"I'm good. It's just the right-hand bleeding" she assures.

"I'm glad you're safe. See you soon."

"It's him. I'm quite sure by now. He isn't in Maine. He never went there."

"Well, I get that, but first, your hand should be the priority," adds Tony.

They hang up the call a few seconds later.

It takes her a week to heal the wound from the bullet shot on the right. However, her conviction and positive attitude helps her recover soon. A week later, she shows up again at the headquarters. Her right arm rests on arm support by her shoulder. She sips her tea and watches the outline of the morning sky from her window space. She smiles at her past feelings, grateful to the savior for saving her life.

CHAPTER TWENTY SEVEN

On the Day Before Leona's Death

The breezy morning gets welcoming applause from the alluring oceanfront. Leona Hill sits on her chair in the front yard and takes a glimpse of the panoramic view of the coast. She sips her tea and applies some sugar cubes. Her emotions shift on the day she had an argument with her daughter. She feels sorry and laments the words she used. Now, she misses her in the front yard. Daisy has left for her schooling, and she has never attempted to call her since then. She appreciates how much the weather has changed by now as she ponders the sunny side of the bright day. Far off in the dock, her vision elongates and she finds the keeper nailing on his boat. She keeps and lingers on him for a long time, and never cares about the rest. Her memory doesn't fade as early, and it reminds of her husband and how he used to do the same. That's a long time ago. Her little brain convinces it.

In the distance, she witnesses the arrival of a car and stops at her gate. She feels the surge of something imprecise. She gets on her feet and waits to see who comes out of the car. Leona recognizes her instantly and finds it odd. Julian Baker walks off to her and stands as tall as she can to appear confident and intimidating.

"I want the chronicle," she says.

"What are you talking about?" Leona implies.

A sense of wrath emerges upon her. "I'm not here to play a game. You know exactly what I'm talking about," Julian says in fury.

"I don't have it."

"You don't deserve the money. He was my husband, who was murdered by your fucking daughter."

Leona listens to her patiently and then implies herself as well as she can to make it look softer. "It was the deal."

"Not about the money mentioned in the chronicle."

"We deserve it as much as you do. My daughter risked her life, and now she's under suspicion. You know what it means."

"I don't care about that. Get me my chronicle," says annoying Julian.

The altercation escalates, and the keeper marks his presence to cease between the two. Julian Baker looks at him very intimately, as if they have some kind of blood relationship. This makes a fuss for Leona Hill. It gives her dubious thoughts, and she finds it quite relevant.

"This is not the end," Julian warns.

She walks with the keeper toward the lighthouse. Leona stands and watches her go inside the attic.

"Are they related?"

It baffles her. Thirty minutes later, she finds them both outside, and Julian leaves the coast and speeds with her car. Leona is curious. "How do they know each other?" She walks toward the dock where the keeper is fixing his boat. The bright day shimmers with the sunny side of the day, with a gradual uproar of heat from the oceanfront. The humidity is rising in the air.

"How do you know her?"

Amos turns his back and stands on his feet. He glares at her, and then drops his hammer on the dock and gets close to her.

"She used to be my teacher."

"What kind of teacher?" she asks.

"That's none of your business."

"Is it? She looked at you very intimately. You both know each other for a long time."

"Like I said, she was my teacher."

Leona finds it very tough to get convinced by the man, and then gives up her effort to further question the keeper. She assumes it to be some foul play and keeps it to herself for the moment. She returns with no ramifications. This aftermath has put more uncertainty about the keeper, and in time, she feels a misleading deception being conspired against her.

When the dusk falls, the lighthouse is abandoned by the keeper. He leaves for Brooklyn. An hour ago, he received a call from Daisy to be there by the next day. He leaves by the night and the lighthouse stands empty and dark with no signs, its beam focusing the oceanfront. Leona stands in her front yard and watches the darkness engulf the coast. She feels the breeze rushing through her skin. A sense of foul play creeps into her mind. She is petrified and attempts to take a look at the lighthouse. Indeed, the keeper is missing. She returns after a brief examination along the dock and takes charge of lighting her yard. She waits for the morning, thinking about the chronicle. Though she faintly knows about it, the details still elude her. She hasn't seen the chronicle yet, nor the terms and the money that Julian talked about. Long ago, she heard about it from the Statesman, but now her memory fails to restore the cause. Somehow, the woman spends her night in solitude thinking about her daughter. She tries to make a connection, but it is in vain with every attempt. And then she realizes her cruel intention of killing her daughter for her safety. As this thought surfaces, it becomes clear that the keeper is cunning and clever on all sides. He's in the upper hand.

When the clock strikes midnight, she wakes up and turns on the television. Prepares herself a cup of ginger tea, covers herself with a shawl, and settles on the couch. She watches the highlights of the President's debate for the upcoming election. She sips and lingers on the screen; in between, the fear rises, and sneaks out through the window searching for the presence of the keeper. It daunts her even more, and she feels a scarcity of livelihood in the surroundings. She walks out into her front yard for a while, and then wades in again. The television keeps her busy with the uninteresting debate over the campaign. She takes another cup of ginger tea to keep herself awake and reflects on the day's bad end. The fuss is evident on her face as she can't calm herself over the entire drama that she has been a part of. She keeps trying again to connect to her daughter but fails, and in distress, she throws the phone away, shattering it into pieces. She becomes more suspicious about the keeper, which makes her feel discomfort. Now, her fear shifts to her daughter's life. She can feel the uneasiness crawling up her spines as she imagines the presence of the keeper with her daughter. The picture vividly imprints on her mind, unsettling her. She gets frustrated, disheartened, and at the same time clueless about any assistance.

When the night shifts and the dawn breaks, Leona feels the shimmer of sunshine intruding into the house. She opens her eyes steadily. She finds the break of day but hasn't seen the arrival of the keeper. She repeats the same routine as the night and waits for him. She prepares her mind to be ferocious and hostile towards the keeper. She gathers courage, thinking of herself as a person of power and strength. She waits and strolls toward the coast, returns again, and sits in her front yard, sipping tea more often. The wait can't be any longer, as she finds the day's end slanting toward the west. She twitches in the direction of the road and keeps her ears clear to perceive any vehicle sound. This time, she gets it right; a truck seems to cross the road, but it isn't the man she's looking for. It's her neighbor from a distance. She waves at the man, and he waves back.

In Brooklyn, the keeper learns about the chronicle from Daisy. He has brief information about it, and when the sun gets down, he sets off to return. On the way, he makes a call to Julian Baker and shares the details about the chronicle that she's looking for. The keeper promises Daisy to rescue her from the confinement. She trusts him and waits for the day to come.

Amos, the keeper, halts in the darkness of the oceanfront and opens the door of the attic. He settles in for the night and keeps the tower lamp off. He dismisses the rest of his activities and goes to bed with plans to start fresh in the morning.

When the dawn breaks and the bright sunshine shoots out, Amos finds Leona Hill in his attic. That's where the altercation begins, and she becomes captive under the attic roof.

Few days later, the keeper informs about the death of Leona Hill to Julian Baker. That brings a smile to her face. She summons his presence in Maine. A day later, the keeper makes his errand and meets the woman. Julian Baker seems to be desirous about the chronicle and the money, as she's frightened about the other partners who hold the same right. She craves details from the keeper, and warns him that nothing should surface in the open.

The keeper returns with her. Julian Baker feels the need to search Leona Hill's house. She does that on the day they return to the Island. She finds nothing and presses the keeper to ensure Leona is dead. She visits the place where Leona is buried. When the sun goes down, she prepares to leave him.

"You have a duty to do. Get the chronicle from the girl," she insists.

"I will."

"Take care. You're like my son."

Julian Baker drives away.

In the far distance from the road, away from the chaos, the Sheriff observes keenly. He finds the situation strange and unusually odd. He doubts the keeper and the woman, whom he has never seen, making it even more uncertain. He turns his car and then sets his footprints in his office to find out about the woman. The unconfirmed relationship between them lingers in his mind.

CHAPTER TWENTY EIGHT

The Unresolved Chaos

"What do you say about this unresolved chaos? It's getting on my nerve," says Susan.

Tony hoists his head from the monitor.

"Good to see you back. Is that arm support helping you?"

She shrugs. "Sort of."

"Well, the chaos is getting even bigger. Be prepared to be surprised."

She looks at the database of citizen details. The discovery is real and for sure a heart-wrenching truth to be revealed.

"What's the chaos here?"

"It turns out, the keeper, or Amos Cott, is actually Isabella Cott, the daughter of Julian Baker."

"You mean to say, the daughter of Blanford Sky."

Tony nods. "That's the reason she went missing, because she knew we would discover the truth."

"I always doubted her from the beginning. And it became more certain when the Sheriff shared about a woman with the keeper. Well, the mirror is clear now."

"Was Isabella abandoned by her parents?"

"I can't say no to that. Blanford Sky kept his relationships with women a secret."

"Certainly Julian Baker is not the first woman."

"We go for the head," adds Tony.

"What did the press write?"

"Have a look for yourself."

Susan picks the New York Times, and the headline in black typeface reads, "The Unresolved Chaos of the City Still Remains Cluttered." She sips the tea offered to her and drops the newspaper.

"I wonder how they come up with those words."

"That's why it's called journalism," Tony says with a wide expression in his eyes.

"See you later," Susan says as she exits the door.

On a summer night, when the breeze is silent, cool, and calm, Blanford Sky is blessed with a daughter. When he sees the face of his wife, he doesn't seem to be joyful about the new life. Julian Baker lies asleep, with her eyes closed and deprived of vitamins in her body. She hears the cry of the newborn baby, which wakes her up, and gathers some strength to look at her daughter. Her joyful face radiates a glorifying triumph, a victory she has craved for years. She holds the crying baby in her arms. The nurses in the ward help her to sit up. Julian caresses her daughter. Blanford stands aside and leans on the bed.

"Congratulations."

"To you as well," says Julian.

It isn't the same that Blanford feels. Somewhere in his mind, he primarily disregards the child as his own. The reason – he desired a male child, which seems far from his reality. He concludes in his mind not to accept the child. His male dominance allows him to be more autocratic toward the woman.

"You're happy?" he probes.

"Aren't you?"

He doesn't say any words but reflects his feelings through his actions. He gets on his feet, kisses his wife's forehead, and walks out of the ward room.

"Where are you leaving?"

"I've got business to do," he says, then leaves.

Julian feels the ignorance of him being a father to the child. She expresses her concern and becomes exasperated at his conduct. As time passes, days turn into years, and Isabella Cott grows up deprived of her father's love. When she starts to understand why her father didn't accept her, she realizes it's because she isn't the son he desired. Julian Baker begins to follow as a single parent in raising her. This leads to many arguments and brawls between them.

A week after the arguments, the Statesman applies for foster care, deliberately against his wife's wishes. He controls the power, and nothing can be assessed against the man. Julian surrenders and tries her best not to commit any offence against their daughter.

"Please don't do this. She's our daughter," she begs him.

"I'm sorry, darling, I can't help it."

"You will be sorry for this," she says sternly.

"Well, if that's so, let's face it."

A week after they a file petition for foster care, Isabella Cott finds parents in Detroit who want to raise her. However, Julian Baker doesn't leave her daughter. Each weekend, she visits the house to fulfill the need for a genuine mother. She pours love and care. The unnatural chaos, however, puts an impact on Isabella Cott's life. She had seen her father and mother quarrel each night about her being a girl child. Despite this, she thought someday Blanford Sky would accept her as his own. The desire remained unfulfilled. She begins to learn and grow, her conduct surprises all. She displays more dominant traits, revealing more traditionally male characteristics.

Taken aback by the habits of the girl, Julian decides she will treat her daughter the right way. When she begins to speak, she tells and shares all the bad things she has seen in the past. Her foster parents care about her, but the intentions of Isabella Cott remain unpredictable. On one weekend, she shares her thoughts with her mother during her visit.

"I feel like I'm a boy."

Julian laughs at first, not quite seriously, and takes it as an insignificant confession.

"You're my sweet girl, honey. You can't be like other boys."

"But I like being a boy. Even dad wanted a boy."

It sounds quite serious as of now. Julian looks into her eyes and begins to contemplate her.

"What are you talking about?"

"Yes Mom. I want to be a boy. Dad will accept me then."

She's messed up. Julian Baker cogitates.

Julian Baker walks through the hallway to see her husband. She comes in without a knock at the office. Finds his absence on the desk. She waits and takes a seat. Second turns into minutes, when then a woman surfaces from the secret chamber. She's here to talk about the freakish behavior of their daughter. The woman takes her steps one at a time, and her eyes speak of deep concern. Julian gapes with her eyes wide and sees her exit the door. Blanford walks out of the chamber.

"Who's she?"

"What are you doing here?" he says in rage.

"You didn't answer my question."

"It doesn't matter anymore."

She senses the presence of disloyalty, a betrayal of her honesty. She floods in annoyance, a wrath she holds for then. She walks out of the workplace, sobbing with her red, teary eyes. Her feelings get distorted, hurt, and she rages in furious concern. She preserves the resentment and contains it calmly. Her only concern now is her daughter. In a few days, she will visit her again. The incident brings her into deep melancholic constraints, so she goes to look for the woman. In days, she finds out about her.

On a bright morning of the summer month, Julian Baker pays her visit to Leona Hill at Long Island. But, before she gets to meet her, she gets the account of her daughter running away from foster care. She keeps her at home before she drops by. And a week later, she finds about her mental instability and admits her to a rehab center. Isabella Cott begins to learn her own way in the rehabilitation center and gets fonder of being a boy. She learns the hard way to accept herself. With love and care from her mother, she begins to cope with her circumstances. However, Isabella Cott begins to feel that her biological mother wouldn't let her be the person she desires. The first time she runs away from foster care, she lands up in the streets, where she finds a refuge from a couple. She begins to consider them as her adoptive guardian, for they were nice to her.

Julian knocks at the door and stands calm. When the door opens, she finds the woman. The hesitation is seen on the face of Leona Hill.

"Forgive me. I wasn't meant to."

"I'm not here to discuss those trivial matters. I need you to do me a favor."

"What favor?"

"I need you to kill him for me. You will have your share of interest."

Leona raises concern about it. She is terrified and numb at the same time.

"But why do you want to kill your husband?"

"That's none of your business to know," says Julian.

"I can't help you with that."

Leona denies it and shifts toward the kitchen, pouring a glass of water.

"I can pay you whatever the hell you want. Think about it. Here's my card."

Julian Baker leaves her.

The conundrum enlarges in her mind as Leona picks up the card. She's in a state of devastating business. The hunch of uncertainty arises.

"How can I trust this woman?" she wonders.

A few days later, she makes the call. In the years that go by, Julian Baker traces Isabella Cott in the street, helps her daughter financially, and she gets what she desires. She's no longer Isabella Cott, but a newly born man, calling himself Amos Cott. Ever since, he has never remembered his father, the slain Statesman, Blanford Sky.

CHAPTER TWENTY NINE

The Lighthouse Keeper

Susan breathes as she appreciates the view before her eyes. She gazes at the stretching ocean water. The morning is welcomed with a beautiful array of songs from the gulls. The swells lap and hover in and out of the coast. She isn't alone on the Island. She has the company of her friend, Massy Paul.

"What a beautiful place," describes Massy.

"It used to be, but not now."

She nods her head. "Sorry about that. I know the story," adds Massy.

Then they trudge inside the attic where the keeper lived. It's empty, and a smell hovers on the closed wall. It appears to be the same as how they left it before closing the site.

"Do you see those marks in the wall?"

Massy raises her head and tries her best to read them well. "Yes, I do."

"Those were engraved during the war. The soldiers spent their days counting on them."

Massy takes a closer look as her feet wade, pushing herself to the wall. She runs her palm and feels the marks and symbols. It's hard and steady as hell. Strong and well-built.

"Does the keeper know of all those?"

"I'm not quite sure."

"Here's a thing: is the keeper a guy or a girl?"

Susan giggles at her. "A transsexual man. He used to be Isabella Cott."

"That's gross."

They walk out of the attic and spend an hour on the dock watching the oceanfront. Up in the sky, the gulls are returning for their inhabit. When the sun overheads them, they return to the city. Susan drops her at the bar before she embarks on. She exhibits some sense of clarity by now and feels the knock on her gut about the unsolved mystery. She stops her car at the entrance of the headquarters. She walks confidently and nonchalantly. A familiar face walks by, with no heed or attention given. She halts instantly and turns back to find out the figure. The woman exits the door, and only a part of her side face reveals itself to her. "That's Julian Baker," she mutters to herself. She appears intrigued and curious about the woman's presence. She takes the elevator and knocks straight at Tony's room.

"I just saw Julian."

"So, you did encounter her."

"What was she here for?" Susan enquires.

"Obvious reason. She wants to know the murderer of her husband."

"Did you tell her the truth?"

"That would be an act of foolery."

She nods and takes a glass of water. She shares about her morning visit to Long Island. The keeper goes missing. The conundrum remains the same. She exits the door quite confidently and trudges to her workplace. She devises a plan of execution to move to Maine. The end isn't far, she thinks.

When Julian Baker walks through the aisle, all at once, a sudden silence falls from all. None had anticipated her presence when she showed up at the front door of Tony. She knocks as usual and conducts herself in a manner that is well done. Something odd reflects on her, he senses it. She stands and takes the seat.

"What about the girl?"

It's hard to comprehend her, for she changes like seasons. Tony rests his arm on the desk and leans forward.

"That's the question I'm supposed to ask you."

Her expression intensifies, her eye brows squeeze, and she clears her throat.

"What do you mean? I'm here to know about my husband's murderer."

"Mrs. Baker, if you could cooperate, surely the girl isn't that far from our hands."

She exhibits uneasiness and claims that she's supposed to leave early. Her intuition gets clear by now; they are after her son, Amos Cott.

"Do you think I've done all these?" she raises her voice in anger.

"I don't doubt you. It's just a protocol to suspect."

"And you're wrong in that."

She gets on her feet, her eyes don't blink for even a second, and she looks at him rigidly. She exits and walks faster to catch the elevator. She reckons with the opinion put forward and establishes a new intention as she crosses the foyer. She declines to look around and passes Susan Kelly, who seems to be on her way up.

On her desk, Susan figures out the timely operation she will require to act against the keeper. She's calculative and draws a map of the man's following. Then there is a probable chance of getting away from them. Since the murder of Daisy Collins, Amos Cott has been absconding from people. He hasn't shown his face or appeared in public. His pretentious character reveals the much bigger game he's up to. Firstly, the three murders, and then the attack on Susan. It was quite a lucky escape, and she feels grateful to her savior. As she frames her schemes to plot the game, she gets a call from her close friend.

"What's up?"

"Your mother seems to be worried about you," says Massy.

"She must have seen the accident."

"Why don't you call her?"

"I'm busy right now."

Massy breathes and then sips a glass of wine. "Are you coming today? We got some new arrivals."

"New arrival?"

"I mean new shots."

"I'll see. I've got to go."

Susan cuts the call. She gets the hunch of the entire hatch that Amos Cott will never show up again in the lighthouse. It's seized and under the constant surveillance of the town's Sheriff. But she gets it wrong. When the sun sets, she shows up at the bar and makes a call to her mother.

A week later, Amos Cott feels the breeze, strokes water from the dock, and rubs his hand over his boat. He misses going on his long errand in the deep water, catching salmon for the evening. He breathes out, gets a cigarette from his left, and lights it. He can feel the silence and emptiness prevailing in the setting. His whereabouts seem to be unknown, he thinks so. The graves are no more, and the lighthouse tower is sealed. The attic is locked, and the lamp never glows anymore. It's always dark at night. In the distance, he hears the siren wail. He's sure of the Sheriff. He gets noticed by him as his wailing car approaches closer. The car halts in the dunes. His heart pumps rapidly. The Sheriff unfastens his seat belt, pulls out his gun, and commands in a loud voice.

"Kneel before I shoot."

He gets closer to the dock and takes his footsteps one at a time. He waits for the response of the keeper. He sets his feet steady and is ready to pull the trigger whenever necessary.

A brutal laugh unveils itself from Amos Cott. He turns his face and puffs his cigarette. Then he takes a step ahead but gets warned by the Sheriff.

"It's good to see you, my friend," says Amos.

"If I had known you're a murderer, you wouldn't be standing here now. You fucking bitch."

"So, you know about my past."

"I know you, Isabella Cott," says the Sheriff, intensely.

He gets closer to him and tends to grab him by the arm. Amos escapes the first attempt and then walks away from the dock. He gets into the dunes.

"You can't arrest me, Sheriff. You can't."

The Sheriff stands steady, pointing his gun at him. He listens.

"C'mon, Amos, you know that's a crime."

"Don't act kind, Sheriff. I know my rights."

He gets away from the dry dunes, hopping ahead toward the road. The Sheriff stands, warning him of the consequences. He shoots at him, but misses his leg. Amos quickly takes position and hides in the bushes. He gets a pistol from his boot and retaliates at him. The Sheriff gets shot in the leg and limps to the ground.

The savage laughs and breaks free of him. "Your time is near, Sheriff," he shouts and fades in the darkness.

CHAPTER THIRTY

The First Show at Broadway

The streets shines and radiates with colors of light. Amos watches people as he stands on the sidewalk. He's in Times Square, reading the bulletin where words run one after another. He gets a hunch about the crowd and walks away from the mob. His photo displays prominently on the big screen as a runaway fugitive. Some people watch it, while others don't pay attention. His intention remains the same since morning: he gets a ticket for a show at the Broadway theatre. It's the first show since the Mayor announced its reopening. He walks, burns a cigarette, and observes people through his hoodie. He waits at one point and enters a public restroom. When it gets empty, Amos closes the door of a private stall. He feels dizzy, lame, and fragile. From his left pocket, he fetches a syringe, and from the right hand, he gets a small vial. He injects the hormones and waits. He falls on the floor, slightly mellow, and waits to regain his strength. When done, he gets out and walks ahead to the show.

The presence of the horde makes it difficult to lower his hoodie. He doesn't want to be recognized, so he maintains it. He waits in the queue at the entrance. He hears from behind that Mayor will attend the show on opening day. Silent and speechless, he keenly observes people. An hour later, the city Mayor arrives, and Amos gets a close look at the man, fixing his face in his mind. The proceedings begin, he enters the theatre, and gets his seat right in the middle of the row.

Halfway through the play, Amos realizes the theme of the drama. It's a replica and iteration of exactly what happened at the lighthouse. His spine chills as the show continues. He starts to feel guilty about his decision and perceives it as a bad experience. He keenly watches himself, the person he once was, the keeper on the Island. The actor on stage pulls of a reflection of his own self, the savage being he sees himself as. The portrayal depicts Amos, tagging him as a murderer by the end of the show. He watches until the curtain falls.

Outside, the drizzle grooves in the air, and he feels the satire interpretation of the shcw, finding himself to be the murderer. Amos stands in a shade to stay dry, fetches a cigarette from his right pocket, and lights it. There's a slight whine of breeze crossing the city streets. He puffs and waits for the drizzle to stop. Away from him, a shoplifter is being chased by the police for stealing money from a store. He observes the chase and walks away from ordinary life.

To spend the night, he visits Daisy's apartment in Brooklyn. The room has been the same since his last visit to rescue her. He looks for dinner preparations in the kitchen and finds some bread and milk in the refrigerator. The television still works, and he puts on the bulletin, then switches to entertainment. Amidst the safe night, he's unable to forget the show, his portrayal as the worst keeper, the murderer. It haunts him in the corner of his mind. The show has become a hit in days. It's the first show he has attended in his entire life.

As he eats the pieces of bread and drinks the milk on the couch, a knock comes clear. It sounds rough, and a tantrum seems to be part of it. The old coarse voice is audible enough to wake the neighbors. Amos walks slowly in, and the voice gets even louder as he reaches the door.

"Who is it?"

"I need the rent."

He opens the door for the landlady. The old lady stands on her support. She feels pesky and unattainable to the man.

"Where's Daisy?" asks the landlady.

"She's not here. She's gone home."

The lucid lie seems convincing.

"Tell her when she comes. I need the money."

Amos watches her walk upstairs and shuts the door. The next morning, before dawn breaks, he sneaks out of the apartment and flees to Maine. He carries the roll of the chronicle with him. On his way, he gets a call from his mother.

"You shouldn't be spending more time in the city," says Julian Baker.

"I'm on my way."

Though he's far behind the city's existence, he still can't let go of the show he watched the day before. It lingers on his thoughts and mind, and at times brings a shiver down his spine, imagining the future prospect of his survival. He's everywhere now, just like Daisy, whom he once knew well. And that everything turns against him. He feels the encirclement of his world dragging down upon him. Caged in walls and being persecuted in front of many eyes. He begins to feel strange about it, and fear surfaces on his face.

The train ride to Maine gives him a hard schedule, and the cold air crushes him, squeezing like wet clothes in the sun. The ordinary world sets him apart from the rest, and how he laments over his deed seems to be inconvertible; the guilty is punishable, he knows it well. He mourns in solitude at one corner of the train, where a few travelers are seen. The dead faces flash before him, and the vision of a fearful apparition appears to shake his world. He crawls more inward to protect himself with the hoodie he wears.

An hour later, the whistle blows, and the brakes cringe onto the wheels of the speeding train. It comes to a halt. The station appears deserted and lonely. He doesn't feel like getting out of the coach. He's in Maine. The ticket master arrives and greets him.

"Sir, you've reached your destination," says the ticket master.

He fumbles and gazes at him in dread. Amos breathes and gets himself ready to walk out of the coach.

"Thank you for reminding."

He covers himself with the shawl he had borrowed from Daisy's apartment and covers his head with a hoodie. He takes his first step toward the station platform. He feels the cold breeze rushing against him. Then, a minute later, he watches the train leave. It's returning to Brooklyn. He waits in the deserted station for a while at one corner. Seated on a cold pew, he gapes and ponders hard. He fetches his last piece of cigarette from his right pocket and burns it. It keeps him warm for a little while. "What am I gonna do?" he wonders. On his last puff, he receives a call from his mother.

"It's been four hours. You should be here by now."

Amos clears his throat and throws away the remains of the cigarette.

"I'll be there soon," he adds.

"You should protect yourself from the cold. Don't let anyone find you."

"I'm protected. You don't have to fret about my identity."

"I expect you to bring the chronicle."

"I didn't find it. It must have been buried with her," says Amos.

The raw lie escalates displeasure for Julian Baker. She gets on her nerves and starts pounding on him.

"Don't fool me. You're not a good liar. I know every blood of yours, Isabella."

"I'm no longer Isabella."

"Maybe for people, but to me, you're the same."

Amos hangs up the call. He breathes, sighs with a heavy heart, and stands on his feet. He twitches in both directions, scans the perimeter, and finds no one around. He takes his first step in the cold and marches toward home. On his left shoulder, he hangs a rug with a few of his stuff mounded in it. He feels unwelcome and walks to the front porch of the house, where he sees white flowers blooming brightly. It reminds him of the days that he spent in the lighthouse. He misses fixing his dock and going out into the deep ocean. And here he stands as a fugitive.

He makes his fist and knocks at the door. He breathes and waits, thinking about the chronicle he has. It is the only secret he has been concealing from Julian Baker. The door opens for him. There's a facile smile that he receives from her, and he walks in.

This ordinary world begins to haunt him each night for days. The dead faces come as dreams, as fearful as they seem to be in the real world. Amos keeps it secret to himself along with the chronicle, the money, and the scheme about assassinating the President.

CHAPTER THIRTY ONE

The Chinese Benefactor

The Hotel Grande Albergo delle Palme gets its first visitors since the shootout. The press queues up for visitors who are about to enter the hotel for their stay. Cautionary steps are taken within the perimeter, and none from the outside will be allowed to enter without prior permission. Among them, a Chinese benefactor books suite number thirteen on the fourth floor. His purpose clearly reflects the intent of his visit to the States, solely for the chronicle of a distant friend and partner of the slain Statesman. On the day he's supposed to land, it has been raining since morning. The street appears hazy, and pits get logged with water in different areas of the road.

He gets out of the car and opens up his umbrella. The blizzard continues as he walks toward the shed, the entrance of the hotel. He's surrounded by the press from all channels. The questions pour from every direction. The same type.

"Sir, why did you choose suite number thirteen again?"

The Chinese benefactor didn't quite get the query. He spoke in Mandarin, and no one was able to follow him. He gets his interpreter on the line and converses. He later speaks for himself in the language of the people, so-called English. He desires to speak about the purpose of his visit in a brief manner without concealing the truth behind it. His reasons stand out as he talks about suite number thirteen.

"I like mystery," says the Chinese benefactor.

He seems to be comical at times, which makes the complexity even more rigorous to be around. The press gets a little of the man as he is escorted by the hotel attendant. He walks the elegant foyer of the hotel, gambles on his feet, scans the entire lobby, and praises the décor of the designs hung on the walls. The benefactor gets his suite key and directs himself toward the elevator. Before embarking on the elevator, he gets a welcome drink. It's Arthur again who is in charge of the suite. He cares for the guest who arrives in the suite. He helps the benefactor with the luggage. On the fourth floor, the elevator stops. The benefactor walks out and follows Arthur. The hallway appears enormous.

"I'm Arthur, Sir. I'll be your caretaker."

The benefactor looks at him, as if he's examining him thoroughly. Again, the language borders them. He replies in Mandarin. Arthur uses his translation machine and follows the benefactor.

"I'm Arthur, Sir. I'll be your caretaker," he repeats again.

"I'm Fen Li. Nice to meet you."

Arthur finds he speaks English, which amazes him.

They walk the long hallway and pass a few suites. The walls are newly decorated with paintings and artefacts. Fen Li stops at one point and asks the bellboy about it.

"Do you sell them?"

Fen Li points at one.

"No sir. It's only for decorative purposes."

He follows Arthur again. "How far?"

"Just one more turn," assures Arthur.

Fen Li waits behind as the door of the suite opens. He walks in. The fragrance saturates inside and allures the hall. It turns massive as he wades deeper into the suite. Then he finds the paintings and artefacts. The gallery has several portraits of medieval history. He shuffles toward the rack and takes a close look at the clay teapot and the jars. The breeze slithers through the window and gets his vantage point outside the garden. He turns back and takes a thorough look at the entire suite.

"This is where the Statesman was murdered, am I right?"

"You're right, sire," Arthur nods his head.

"I like the décor of the suite and the smell of it."

"I hope you have a good stay, sire."

Arthur offers him tea in a crystal glass and cookies from the jar. The rain hasn't stopped. The thunders and lightning rigorously testify to the earthly mortals.

"Can I smoke?"

"Yes, you can. You're not prohibited from it."

"Thank you for your service," says Fen Li, a sort of kindness that reflects on him.

Arthur expects a reward from the man, but his hope dies out very fast. He isn't the man from France. He's from China and he thinks of him as a bona-fide niggard. He has to walk out of the suite empty. The earnings would have added to his extra income for the day.

At night, Fen Li stares out of the window and smokes his pipe. The traditional man claims to be an expert in martial arts and waits for the break of dawn. He significantly keeps himself strong and progressive with his early gain from the martial arts. The rain has shrunken down for a while, and the night's tempest crawls in as it gets clear.

At dawn, Fen Li is seen in the garden in his martial arts attire. The man stands strong and stiff as he completes his routine. Arthur watches him very closely. He's there for the day to serve the benefactor.

"Will you teach me some moves, sire?"

Fen Li smiles as he grabs the glass of mango juice. He drinks it quickly and sits on the pew. Arthur gets to join by his side.

"But this brings no money to you, boy."

Arthur is meek at his behavior. "I want to learn to protect myself."

Fen Li looks at him. The intense enthusiasm reveals itself in his face. He then smiles at the boy and says, "Come over."

The bellboy takes a few lessons from the Chinese man. As the daylight breaks from the east, they walk through the hallway to suite number thirteen. Fen Li gets inside his suite. The bellboy waits outside for him to lead him to the dining hall. Thirty minutes later, Arthur sees the man walk out of the suite in his most fashionable attire.

"Are you going somewhere, sire?"

"Yes, Arthur."

"Will I see you again?"

Fen Li ceases and kneels on his knee to look into the eyes of the bellboy. He seems innocent and demure.

"Remember what I taught you this morning."

The bellboy nods. He escorts him to the dining hall. At quarter past eleven, Fen Li walks out of the hotel. A car waits for him outside. His intention gets refined, and it bothers him only about the chronicle. The entire stakeholder community and the benefactors seem to be in the race for the money. From the suite, Arthur looks at him and waves his hand. Fen Li watches the boy before getting inside. He has a briefcase in his left hand and waves with the right. Then he gets inside the car and sweeps off in the bright day to Long Island.

While cleaning the suite, Arthur finds an envelope on the tea table that reads, *For Arthur*. He picks it up and opens it, only to find dollar bills for his service. The boy cries in joy, owning it for himself, and the happy boy once again loves his job.

Susan Kelly follows the man. Fen Li has been under scanner since his arrival at the hotel. Not on a suspect case, but his safety measures mattered the most. Though the detective has been under cover, she hasn't appeared before the benefactor at any given chance. It's all a confidential operation.

Fen Li stands on the road and watches the coast from a vantage point. The lighthouse stands tall and huge. He sees the yellow barrier tape surrounding the perimeter. Then he turns his heels and wades toward the house. The coast appears serene and deserted. He sees a few gulls flying atop the tower. He feels the calmness and walks into the picket fence house. The yard has been dry, and newly wild ferns have grown within the days. Fen Li stands stiffly and knocks with his fist. Once, twice, thrice, the response remains unanswered. He looks around and finds none. He pushes the door. It creaks, and his steps follow.

"Is there anyone else here?"

His tone echoes, but none care to revert back. He finds the dismantled couch, the tables, and the television untouched for quite some time. He turns back and wades out. He looks around. The surrounding perimeter is quiet and silent. As he wanders around, Fen Li hears the sound of a wailing car. The Sheriff arrives.

"How can I help you, sire?"

He shows the address and the photograph of the woman. "I'm here looking for this woman."

The Sheriff takes it from him and shakes his head. "I'm sorry, sir, you'll have to leave."

"But I need to find this woman."

"She isn't here anymore."

"What happened?"

"She was murdered."

Fen Li breathes out and sighs. He takes a last glance at the forbidden lighthouse and returns to the hotel. He doesn't waste any more of his valuable time and gets to the airport. Susan follows him, distinctly in disguised fashion. She watches him from a distance. Alan stands beside her.

"He seems sad."

"I know. He lost the money."

Fen Li disappears from their sight. He feels sorry for the Statesman and then losing the money makes it appalling.

CHAPTER THIRTY TWO

A Cold Day in Maine

The frost stagnates on the damp grasses, and the dew on the ground crystallizes and appears white. The breeze comes from the northern Atlantic. It's chilling and crispy as well, as it hits the skin of a white and black man walking across the streets. The keeper sleeps, unaware of the happenings, and his peaceful and glorious face reflects. The fireplace keeps him warm, but the heat from it makes sure he doesn't get to know about the break of the day. Lost in the intense tiredness of the day, he dreams of all the good things. He has left the chronicle on his desk, revealing all of it. There are no second thoughts of it to be concealed from all.

Julian Baker walks in and finds him asleep as usual. She wades toward the fireplace and warms her hand. She's here to wake the keeper for the day's errand in the nearby woodland. She clears her throat and gives a hint about her presence, but Amos, least aware of it, remains invariant to his senses. She shuffles toward the window and peeks outside. It's cold and frosty in the air. She intends to walk out of the room, and to her conscious appeal, she comes across the desk where the chronicle lies unfolded. She handpicks and harvests what's on the sheet of paper. She meticulously goes through it and leaves it in the same spot. She throws a last glance from the corner of her eyes and leaves him. And then she waits for the keeper to be awake. She gets ready for the woodland and sips mint tea on her veranda, watching the cold day.

"I'm ready."

The voice catches her attention. Amos wakes up in his attire and is ready for the day's errand to collect wood for the evening from the nearby forest. He covers himself with woollen clothes and a shawl to beat the cold, then burns a cigarette to keep himself warm.

"Let's walk through the cold," says Julian Baker.

The former attorney seems to be susceptible to the presence of her transsexual son. Though she never expresses it, but that morning she feels it because the disregard for the chronicle makes it even more prone to the man. Amos burns another cigarette as they walk uphill in the deep forest. Then they halt at their spot and start their collection of the slender woods for the evening.

"You didn't tell me about your journey?"

Amos throws the last puff away and looks at his mother. He has the smile of an innocent boy. "It was fine. Cold though."

She watches him cut the wood into pieces and stock it in the carrier. The birds chirp in the sky. The dense woods cover the clear sky, and the day's light fails to drop through the canopy.

"How did you rescue Daisy Collins?"

The question never stops coming from the former attorney.

"It was hard. I covered her in a hoodie and then fled to Long Island."

"That's a short explanation of the herculean task."

By evening, they return to their household activities. In the backyard, Amos prepares chicken soup in an old container that is quite rusty and corroded. He supplies more wood to the fire to keep it robust to beat the cold. The daylight has been swapping away, and the frost in the air thickens as it gets darker. In the kitchen, Julian prepares dinner for both. She walks out into the backyard to find him doing the stuff.

"That's a good smell. It reminds me of my grandfather."

"What was he like?"

"He used to be a hunter during the night and a fisherman during the day."

Amos shares a chuckle. "An adventurous old man."

"Indeed."

"And you liked being a lawyer."

She nods.

"Just to make sure, you really don't know where the chronicle is?"

Amos stops fiddling, halts his stirring of the soup, and gets on his feet. He breathes out and then takes a few steps.

"I speak the truth," he says. "It must have been buried with her."

He says the same thing as before.

"Alright."

She bursts in and then, minutes later, calls him inside with the soup. The night grows, and the darkness crawls in. It's getting deeper and deeper. Amos stops putting wood into the fire and keeps it lightly burning. He wades with the soup container and sets it on the table. The dinner table is ready. All set to devour at the same time. Julian pours some wine for herself and then passes it on to her son. She acknowledges her son's effort in the preparation. Amos stays firm and intact with his conviction to not disclose much about the chronicle. He sees her grab a spoon and taste the soup.

"It tastes delicious."

"I hope I didn't mess it up."

He takes his seat, comforts himself, and starts their dinner. The fork lifts certain pieces of meat from the plate, and the smell airs it all. Julian Baker sips her wine and gives a close glance at him, fairly in a biased manner.

"I used to like the woman you were," she says.

Amos chuckles. "But I never liked my old self."

"Sorry about that. You had a hard time, all of it."

He nods and then sips his wine. The fireplace keeps them warm, and the frosty night turns dense.

"You did love her, right?"

He shakes his head, affirmative. "Yes, I did. I never intended to kill her. It was a grievous mistake that I lament."

"There was no other way. Daisy Collins had to die."

Amos stares at his mother, which is quite daunting and creepy to hear. He didn't think of that coming from her. He pours more wine into his glass and takes a bite of the chicken piece. His mind rumbles around on questions that, for a long time, he had left unheard.

"Why did you kill Father?"

Julian Baker stops fiddling with the fork and drops it on the plate. She sighs heavily, breathing out, then sips her wine to wet her dry throat.

"The man deserved it."

"But why?"

"Because he was cheating on me with the woman you fucked," her tone gets intense.

There's a silence for a few seconds and then it resumes with the dinner talk. He watches her closely.

"You did good today with the woods. But you shouldn't have left the Sheriff alive."

An awkwardness develops between the two. It seems nothing new has been happening since his arrival. Amos finds it hard to answer all of it. But he's obliged to follow all of it. For he knows the share of his hand in the crimes.

"He managed to escape by an inch," he adds in a simplistic way.

"He's a threat. He's the reason we're under the focus of Susan Kelly."

She finishes her dinner and takes a smoke from her pipe for a while to keep herself warm. Then she shifts toward the fireplace. She picks up her wine glass and comforts herself by the fireside. She opens her unfinished book and starts reading with a sip of her red wine. Amos joins by her side and leans on the stone wall. He lights his cigarette and listens to her blabber.

"He's fortunate to have missed my bullet," says Amos and puffs.

When the night begins to freeze, the former attorney, Julian Baker, takes her leave and goes to bed. She walks in her steady motion. She turns her heel to revert to the keeper. He seems to be by the fireside, pushing wood for the night.

"Blanford Sky never accepted you as his daughter. He never loved you the way I did. I did all these for you, for us, and for the money."

She walks into her room.

Amos watches her, and his thoughts divert to her truth. He feels the behemoth of all, squeezing him from all sides as he ponders and discerns to know.

Somewhere in her tiny brain, Julian Baker knows the truth about the chronicle. She remains calm and silent as she waits for the right day to arrive.

CHAPTER THIRTY THREE

The Lost Romance

The bar illuminates in different shades of color. It's the music that keeps engaging the people around, and many find their best time to revitalize their tiresome day. In the corner, the television murmurs, showing the face of the keeper who is a runaway fugitive. The buzz falls easily amongst the people around. The whispers sound clearer, and the talk appears to be real. Susan solicits a beer as she walks in. The dusk arrives with a slight shower from the dark clouds hovering above. She takes her usual counter seat. She sighs heavily. Then she leans backward, facing the television. She feels awkward about the timely presence of people with the inappropriate bulletin. She makes a request if Massy could change the channel to something better. She sounds exhaustive as hell.

"That's so gross all the time," says Susan, pointing at the television.

"All right. I'm switching."

Massy handles the remote control and flips the channel.

"Thanks," Susan sips her beer, "by the way, I loved your mother's house."

"She was asking about you this entire week."

As the daylight fades away, the darkness crawls with people returning from work and entering the bar. Massy gets busy in a while, standing along the beer machine serving the newcomers. Susan taps her fist on the counter as she hums to herself in a series of harmonic tones. She sips in between and watches people through the doorway. A hand taps her back. She turns around, and a familiar face appears. She smiles, and then finds it quite delicate. The man stands tall and substantially fit.

"Hi," says Susan.

"Good to see you," the man says with a defined jawline.

From the machine, Massy watches them closely. The man takes a seat close to Susan. A beer glass drops for him.

"For you," says Massy.

"Thank you."

Susan shares the attribute of the man to her friend. "Massy, that's Daniel Ryan, and Daniel, that's Massy."

"You both look cute together. How do you know each other?"

Susan clears her throat and has the smirk, "We used to date once."

"I knew it. There's something between you both. Give me a second," says Massy.

She attends to the other newcomers and serves them their demands, then returns to them. The conversation doesn't limit anymore. Her curiosity reflects on her face. Susan watches her in a manner that she finds quite embarrassing, though her hormones suggest how content she feels to see Daniel after such a long time. She gestures, eyes raised to contemplate, how she didn't want Massy to mess things up.

"Get me a beer," Susan breaks her voice.

There is a crest of silence between them.

"You must have been dating a lot," adds Susan.

Daniel giggles. "No, not much."

Massy arrives with the beer glass and drops it on the counter. She leans her hand forward and joins them. She utters nothing but pays complete attention, which is awkward for any two people.

"I think you both should date again," says Massy, as she leaves them, smiling. "Just saying."

"She's just being naïve," Susan shrugs.

A week after, Susan gets a call from Daniel. An invitation to a show, unexpected yet sounding merry to her.

"How about a show in Broadway?"

"That would be nice."

She doesn't deny it. Instead, she shows up on the day of the show at Broadway. The new show seems fascinating, and its demand across the city doubles within a week of opening. The avenue gathers the most crowd by the time the day ends. It has become the busiest spot of the city. They wait in queue and gaze at people.

"I'm glad we're doing it."

"Thanks for coming," adds Daniel.

"I never even thought I would see you again."

"But here we are."

She gestures, calm and sober. Not the way she usually portrays herself in uniform.

"I've seen you quite a few times on television."

She has a broad smile. "I sort of got tired of those. The media doesn't leave you behind."

"You're doing great. I'm sure you'll fix the mess."

She laughs. They enter the show.

That night, Susan shares the moment with her friend. Massy sticks to the call, her fascination lingering on.

"Did he kiss you?"

"No. We just went to the show."

"Why didn't you kiss him?"

"C'mon, we just met after a long time," expresses Susan.

"I'm glad you're finally happy again."

"Thanks for always being there, and yes, I hate your beer."

Massy laughs out loud and then hangs up the call. "See you in a week."

Tony finds some lineage connection to Maine. It seems Julian Baker has inherited her grandfather's house. Based on the assumptions he collects, the evidence direct her presence in the state of Maine. So does her son, Amos's. The suspects have been located, his intuition makes it clear to him. He immediately summons Susan Kelly to his office. The morning shimmers bright, and the bright day claims the positive side of the city. She walks through the aisles of cubic desk and trudges inside.

"Don't tell me you located them."

"Indeed, you're right. Julian Baker has a property in Maine that she inherited from her grandfather. I'm not saying I'm hundred percent certain, but the probable evidence suggests so."

Susan takes a look at the catalogue; it seems quite right. The name Julian Baker possesses the property in her name.

"So, what now?"

Tony breathes, sips a cup of mint tea from the pot. "It's time to conduct a press meet. I want every news channel and reporter at the entrance immediately."

"Are you sure you want to do this?"

"Yes!" he shrugs.

When the sun sets, the headquarters entrance gets inhibited by reporters from all channels around New York city. At dusk, Tony walks out, followed by Susan Kelly. The flashes of the lens trigger their eyes. The microphones fixed on their stands, Tony confidently faces the horde. Another round of flash blinds his eyes momentarily.

"That's enough," he commands.

"Let the officer talk," someone from the crowd seems sober with that.

Tony begins to detail. "The evidence and the investigation prove the offender has been hiding in Maine. We're underway to seize whoever it is. The culprit can't escape anymore."

"But who is it?" questions a reporter.

"The details will be shared on our official site. We need your cooperation."

"We can't wait for the culprit, why not now?"

That sounded like an inch of rudeness. The reporters make it firm again.

"That's enough," Susan delivers her voice.

In a minute, the horde disperses from the site.

The phone beeps at night. It's an intelligence information that Tony had been waiting for. He reads, and smiles. "The man in hoodie," he reads further, "from Brooklyn to Maine."

CHAPTER THIRTY FOUR

The Radio in the House

On a cold morning, Amos listens to the radio in his square room. The newscast repeatedly speaks about the murder mystery of the erstwhile Statesman. Then, the name gets into his ear: the prime suspects, *Julian Baker and Amos Cott.* He feels a shiver chilling down his spine. He sits by the fireplace and puts wood into it. He worries, a face of irrelevant tumult condemns him. Then the bounty on them makes it more robust. Now the people are on the hunt, with no route to escape, he thinks. He sweats as he hears more of it, then moves toward the living room, makes it worth seeing on the television. It's all true, which he first ignored. He keeps it silent as he sees himself in a banner adjacent to Julian Baker across the entire State. The walls have been closed, and the way has been refuted to them. It's all under a scanner, each day, each night.

In a few days, Amos sees Maine police looking for them. He watches them from the window, hiding. The entire region is under supervision. He shares the news with his mother.

"You know what needs to be done," says Julian.

Amos locks themselves from the outside of the house in the night when the police patrol is missing. It's to deceive the rest.

"Do you think it's a good idea?"

"Just do what I tell you to do. Don't ask too many questions."

Amos refrains from asking more questions. Though he thinks the bulletin warned them, it's already out of their hands.

On one certain day, an officer knocks at the door. He waits for a response in vain, after finding the door locked. Inside, Amos and Julian remain silent and immovable. Not even their breaths hiss on the call.

"Is there anyone inside?" the police officer implores.

He sneaks through the window but finds none. He gestures to his partner in the car and returns.

A minute later, Amos spies through the window, watching the officer move in the opposite direction. He breathes, feeling a kind of relief, and then makes a quick query to his mother.

"How long do we have to stay like this?"

"That's not in my hands."

"You have no idea how hard it's getting day by day," his voice intensifies.

"We have to live with the choice."

"What choice are you talking about? Getting killed?"

Amos displays his frustration and bangs his fist on the table before trudging into his room. He sits on the bed and gazes at the cold night outside. He drops a few logs into the fireplace, reminiscing about his days as the keeper and the kind of woman he used to be before becoming Amos Cott. "Had I stayed as Isabella Cott, perhaps this day wouldn't exist," he ponders, regretful and lamenting it all. He turns on the radio to keep himself updated.

Their new life begins to shrink within those four walls.

As days pass, nights grow longer, they start to run out of firewood. Meanwhile the cold falls miserably. After dinner, that night, Julian comes knocking at his door.

"We're running of wood. The cold can't be tamed."

"How do we get more?"

"We get out in the cold; the dark night will bless us. Be prepared."

He nods.

The next night, the errand begins. The cold breeze slithers through the skin, and breathing becomes exasperating. Julian Baker drives the truck on the murky road. She observes no one; the silent accompanies them in their purpose. Miles from the house, in the deep forest, the truck stops. Amos puts on his hoodie, covering himself. Julian Baker does the same. The keeper has his axe and a cigarette. He lights one.

"Take a puff."

The former attorney puffs and walks uphill. Deep in the forest, they find fallen trees and bushes. Amos starts his work while the former attorney acts as a shadow to protect him. In the distance, the wolf howls, the birds cry, and the owl watches them from the branches. Julian Baker sets a fire and waits for him to finish. For a while, it keeps them warm.

"We can't take chances. Fill for the entire month," suggests Julian.

"Burn a cigarette," says Amos.

His breath comes in mist. He rubs his cold hands, feeling the warmth of the fire. From the uphill, he perceives the small town glowing bright. After cutting the wood into pieces, he loads them into the truck. Midnight passes, and the wolves are asleep. The crescent moon slides down from their vision. Its glow falls through the canopy, lighting the forest darkness. They quickly load the truck. An hour later, they drive back. However, their unfortunate fate betrays them in an ugly manner. Amos slows down the truck when he sees the siren light glow from the vantage point.

"There's a cop ahead."

They cover themselves as though no one can recognize them. The car arrives closer to them.

"Keep moving slow," Julian orders.

The police stop them.

"Where are you heading?"

"Home," answers Julian.

"What's in the truck?"

"Just wood for the cold."

The officer wades back and inspects. He gets the smell of fresh wood.

"Where are you coming from?"

Julian portrays a candid smile. "From South Bay, Long Island."

The officer looks at both, feeling cynical about them. "Do you have a cigarette?"

Amos feels the jolt. "Yes!" he fumbles.

"Thanks. Well, you can go."

The truck stops at the backyard. The wood is stocked in the warehouse storage. Some are left to burn as they beat the cold night. Amos sits close to the fire, remembering how he didn't want to kill Daisy Collins. He blames the former attorney for all the cause that got him into this mess. In days, it seems they were running out of food and groceries.

CHAPTER THIRTY FIVE

The Suspects Behind the House

The suspects behind the house suffer as they draw closer to their end. Julian inspects the kitchen and the refrigerator, discovering the emptiness of all. Scarcity of food and groceries shatters them, a mayhem that leaves them floundering.

"We need to get some food and groceries," says the former attorney.

Amos looks at her with a starving appetite. "There's only one way we can do this."

Julian makes a call to the nearby store and asks for a delivery from the list she made. She peeps out of the window. The morning dew floats in the air; it's dense and spine-chilling outside. As a suspect behind the house, for her, it's no less than being under house arrest. She turns back to the fireplace as she pours some tea into a cup. She distinctly feels the cold and offers a cup to her son.

"When are the edibles coming in?" inquires Amos.

"Soon."

For the rest of the day, all they do is to wait for the sun to go down.

Tony selects a team for the operation. In the morning hour, he summons Susan Kelly, asking her to be prepared for the immediate move. She gets the hunch of it, and then makes it clear how they are supposed to execute without letting the offender know about their arrival.

"They know about us."

"Of course they do. They have seen themselves on the television," adds Tony.

"What guarantees their presence in Maine?" Susan confirms again.

"Their felony."

"Well, I can't disagree with that."

"To be more precise, the Maine police gave a suspicious concern about a house."

"What house?"

"The house where they are hiding. It's been locked for days."

"Alright," she exits.

"We move by noon."

Susan enters her chamber and makes a call to her friend. The call goes unattended. She leaves a message.

"Hey Massy, if you find Daniel coming by, let him know I'm going for an urgent operation to Maine." She keeps it short. Then prepares herself. She fixes her gun, puts on her boots and uniform. The clock ticks twelve noon. She picks up her shades and stands tall on her feet before exiting the building. She hears the call of their corporal, Tony, administering the team before the operation. Susan stands behind, leaning against the wall of the assembly hall.

"You're late."

"Aye! Aye! Captain," she gestures.

The footfalls begin to disperse, the cars in a row shifting. The team heads out.

"An informant confirms he may have seen both on a cold night returning from Long Island."

"But they haven't been here for quite some time."

"That's what we are going to find out."

Susan drives her Chevy. On the way, she picks up Alan. The daylight has already tilted toward the west. The long journey corresponds to a tiresome day. She hands him a gun.

"What am I supposed to do with this?"

"Just keep it. For your safety."

"I don't need all this. I'm just an informant."

"Do you want to die?"

Alan gapes at her, strangely. "You can't say that, and I don't want to die."

"Then keep it."

He reluctantly accepts the fact that he needs a gun to protect himself. For a long time, silence prevails on the road. By sunset, they are in Maine. There are people from the press when they arrive in town.

"What makes you think they are hiding here?"

One of the reporters instantly catches Tony's sight. He struggles to walk in the horde as they head toward the station building. The Maine police escort them.

"We have concrete evidence," he replies.

Susan follows inside the building. The officer welcomes them in the cold evening. He explains about the house and the strange situation over the last few weeks. Then a call had been traced from the same this morning. One of the finest officer was investigating the matter. Tony listens to the officer and gives his opinion.

"We will wait for the night. Just to be sure about their presence."

"That's a good idea," says one of the officers.

"We can't be ignorant but be precise and specific about the details. There are a lot of neighbors out there."

Susan leans her back on the desk and adds to their conversation as a silent listener. Outside, the sky turns dark, and the cold breeze hovers in the blue mountains far in the woods. Alan keeps himself warm by the fire outside. He doesn't like the idea of keeping a gun; for once, he served the erstwhile Statesman as an assistant, and all he had was a bunch of files in his hand. He fiddles with the gun by the fireside.

"Did you ever shoot anyone?" a voice interrupts.

He raises his head and looks up at the man.

"No, never."

"Did you?"

The officer nods. "It was a headshot."

"You must have felt terrible."

"No. I took it as a job. Do you want a cigarette?"

Alan picks one from his pack and lights it from the firewood.

"Seems like it's your first time in this part of the country."

"Pretty much, you can say," shrugs Alan.

Susan walks out and joins them by the fireplace. She warms her cold hands and then smiles at the officer. He tries to offer her a cigarette, but she denies. She watches Alan fiddling with the gun.

"I told you I can't handle a gun," he says, peeking at her.

"It's just a matter of time before you will be frightened to death," Susan titters.

Julian Baker receives the groceries from the delivery man. The disguised face stands before her. It's an officer from the

Maine police. She briskly picks up the groceries, pays the amount rapidly, and shuts the door immediately.

"Thank you," she says, slamming the door behind her.

"Do call if you need more," the officer shouts from outside.

His spy camera records the woman and a slight part of the house. Julian peeks through the window to find the man gone. Then she resumes her preparation in the kitchen.

At the station, Tony examines the recording. He sees her face distinctly.

"That's her, Julian Baker. We're at the right spot."

Susan nods her head. "Well, it seems you weren't wrong."

On the first day, they put the house under observation to spy on any sort of movement. It seems the offenders are smart enough not to move out of the house. The truck in the backyard stands untouched for days since the errand uphill. From the close vicinity, Tony takes a close look at the premises. He finds the back door of the house open from the backyard.

"That's the truck. I remember the color of it," says an officer.

Tony looks at him. "Are you sure?"

"Yes," says the patrol officer.

"Well, I'm trusting you."

When the darkness crawls in, they return to the station. A fascinating day awaits them next.

CHAPTER THIRTY SIX

The Death on Final Confession

The night seems silent and quiet, as the howling of wolves has diminished from the nearby woods. The dinner is ready, and the table is prepared, ready to be devoured by the earthly eaters. Julian Baker takes her usual seat, while Amos sits straight across from her. He takes a piece of bread on his plate and pours the remains of the wine.

"I hope we don't see this day again," mutters the keeper.

"What do you mean?"

"It's just a good omen I dreamt."

"Well, I'm sorry you had to kill her. I didn't mean to hurt."

Amos suppresses a laugh, the same intention and the savage impression on his face. "She was a nice girl," he adds.

For minutes, the silence hovers, then the attorney breaks the hush. She unfurls her stories of the past, the unknown to all, which at times she sought to reveal. But that night, she beseeches herself from the deliberate affliction that she has been holding for long. She sips her wine and talks.

"I was there in the foyer when the Statesman was murdered."

Amos looks at her, baffled, and stops the piece of bread from entering his mouth.

"What happened then?"

"I saw her walk out of the room. I had been following her, didn't trust her much. I went inside the suite number thirteen only to make sure he was dead. Then I followed Daisy Collins."

"Was it necessary?"

She nods. "It's just that I didn't trust Leona Hill, her mother."

"Why didn't you tell me?"

"I waited for the right time. This is tonight. I'd seen her with the chronicle at the subway station. So, you can't lie to me about it."

Amos sighs hard. "You don't believe me."

"No," says Julian Baker.

She puts the chronicle on the dinner table. Amos acts as though he finds it surprising. Indeed it is, for him. He begins to feel the intense chaos from the other side. Julian Baker has a harsh gaze at him.

"I didn't think....," he fumbles.

"You lied to me, son."

"I was about to tell you," he justifies.

"When? I found it on my own. I knew you had it from the very first day."

He breathes, then feels shallowness of the guilty. "Forgive me."

"You don't deserve forgiveness."

She walks off the table and sits by the fire. Amos steadily vacates the chair and leans against the wall.

"I know I should have told you before. I didn't realize how important this was to you."

The silence breaks. The attorney looks at him, then turns her face facing the fire. "Help put the wood."

"Sure," he sighs.

"It's not your fault."

When the night draws mightier and the cold cramps up the air, Amos lies on his bed, eyes staring at the ceiling. Feet away, the fireplace keeps him warm. In his long memory lane, he visits his childhood madness, how he hated being Isabella Cott, and how much he desired to become a boy; it all came true for him. At times, he imagines himself as the woman he could have been, but it's nowhere near. Serving as Isabella Cott, the keeper, might have given him a different experience. And now, in his solitude, he thinks about what went wrong. This little part of his life, he terms as agony. His friction of thoughts guides him, rumbling across the room, a vision of end he perceives. "Am I the bad person?" he thinks all of it. "I took lives of three people, the demon dwells in me." Somewhere he fails to construe reality and finds himself guilty. He wakes up and sits on the edge of the bed, picks a cigarette from the table, and lights it. His tense face gambles him, his mind quarrels within. He hopes for a narrow escape, and in his mother's presence, it's undue for him to live as easily as he seems to be. His savage smile embraces him, the cruel intention reveals to him the actual reality where he seeks to be. He decides to get rid of the old woman living with him. His fear and terror guides him to protect his subsequent expectations. He knows well that the money could make him filthy rich; then he could leave the country for good. But, with Julian Baker in the scene, the hindrance appears, unattainable of his narrow escape. He steps up by the fire and gazes at its flame as the night conquers with omen of power in the eyes of evil. He heats a razor blade knife, making it look sharp in an intense way. He finalizes his purpose and waits for the night to deliver a fresh cold morning.

When the daylight follows the sunshine, the warmth spreads across the clear sky. The dew has gone, and the bright day liberates joy for the people in the town. Amos heats water in the tub for his mother. He watches her keenly from the narrow slit of the door. Julian Baker sips her coffee and walks in before she washes herself.

"The water is hot, mother," the voice arrives from the bathroom.

"Appreciate that, I'm on my way."

Julian Baker drops her robe on the floor and stands naked. She watches him keenly. Though in the eyes of the beholder, Amos tries to avoid her gaze, but he can't stay away from it for seconds. A short glance at her naked body makes it intense. She walks forth and dips in the tub with hot water. From aside, Amos fetches a wet towel and squeezes it in the water. The woman settles in the tub and waits for the cloth to run through her body. The towel kneads through her back, and the hot water makes her feel comfortable.

"How was the night, mother?"

"It was good. Why are you asking such questions?"

"Just worried about you."

"Don't be. I forgave you."

"Have you thought about the money mentioned in the chronicle?"

"I did," she says.

Amos slowly rises from his posture and fetches the razor blade knife from his rear pocket. He grabs her neck tightly with his hand.

"Amos, what are you doing?" she shouts.

The grip gets tighter and more painful. The attorney begins to struggle. The keeper immerses her in the water, her breath chokes, and she fights to save herself. But the strength of the keeper is no match for her. Then he pulls her out of the water. The sudden rescue makes her feel relief with breath, but then her neck is unable to escape the hold.

"You never loved me, mother. You have used me for your selfish deed."

The anger and grudge surface on Amos's face. The more he feels the anger, the tighter his grip gets. His commotion suggests he is rigid in conviction. He stretches out the blade from the knife, his final attempt making him wait.

"Why?...why?...why did you abandon me?"

His temper heats up, the spirits entangle, and he runs his hand across the throat. The sharp blade slits the throat of the attorney. The blood begins to spill out. He dips her under the water; the color changes from colorless to red. A minute later, he let go of the grip on the neck. The body starts to float. He is drenched and stained by blood of his mother. Tears rush out of his melancholic eyes; the rage gets calm. By the fireside, for the last time, he looks at the chronicle and burns it. He glimpses at his dead mother. "I'm sorry mom," he says and walks out of the door.

CHAPTER THIRTY SEVEN

The Offender at its End

Susan and her team surround the house. The perimeter is secured and exit points are sealed. Every man is prepared to blitz. The press follows them, and the channels begin live telecasts of the incident. It has never happened before, but the public's interest makes it a spectacle. Alan, at one corner, takes his position, pointing his gun toward the door. There is no movement for a while; the silence builds, the fabricated bright day revealing opportunities.

The door creaks as Amos walks out, soaked in blood, with a razor blade knife in his right hand. He takes slow steps and halts after a few strides.

"Stay where you are," an officer orders.

The keeper raises his hands, drops the arm on the ground, and kneels. They take him into immediate custody and put on a handcuff. Susan enters the room, scans around the front yard, then moves to the backyard. The warehouse storage is still filled with wood to beat the cold. She finds blood marks on the floor leading to the bathroom.

"As expected," she says to herself. Susan gets closer to the bathtub. The body floats, and the water is distinctly red. She calls for assistance.

"The woman is dead," she assures Tony, who trudges in. Medical experts arrive, lift the body from the water, and take it for further analysis.

At the fireplace, an unburnt piece of the chronicle remains. Susan takes a close look but remains silent, deeming it of no use. She throws the piece into the fireplace. The press barges in, flashes of the area begin to be captured, making headlines across the state. The corpse is transported to the city. Amos Cott is taken for a hearing in the city court. The judgment will be passed in a week. Susan exits the house, thoroughly checking for any evidence. She walks to the main road, with Tony following behind.

"I'm impressed," he says.

"It's finally over," she breathes. By sunset, they return to the city with the offender. Over the next few days, Amos undergoes strict questioning. He reveals all of it and accepts the charges against him. Somewhere in his heart, it did make him feel unpleasant about killing his mother.

"Why did you kill the attorney?" Susan Kelly asks that question. The keeper looks her straight in the eye. "I shouldn't have," he says.

A week later, the testimony is presented in court, suggesting the truth. The convict is assured, and the sentence is pronounced. Amos Cott receives life imprisonment with an additional five years in a rehab center. The press headlines it early that morning. The New York Times prints: *The Woman in the Lighthouse Will Never Be Seen Again*. The Times Square reflects it on its bulletin board: *The Woman in the Lighthouse sentenced to life imprisonment.* The court adjourns with the final verdict.

He spends the first five years in a rehabilitation center before beginning his prison term. For all he has done, he has no regrets.

But on certain days, from his fractured memory, he imagines the presence of Daisy Collins with him in the lighthouse, the woman he once loved.

Amos Cott still possesses a stranded, savage smile and grabs a cigarette from his right pocket before being transported to his long-term prison. He laughs – *the savage, wicked laugh.*

CHAPTER THIRTY EIGHT

The New Keeper

Susan Kelly stands by the roadside, watching the serene coast. Dusk is about to fall, the gulls are returning home, and in the far-off distance, a cargo ship honks. She feels the breeze and lets it pass by. She knows the end will fall into its place, tumbling before her eyes. She waits for the new lighthouse keeper. She smiles at the familiar face in the distance. Alan walks the dunes. The vantage shoreline appears orange, and she appreciates its glow. The ocean laps in swells. She waits.

"Good to see you again," she says.

"It's been quite a long week."

"Thank you for your service," Susan appreciates him.

"It was great to be an informant," he says, smiling.

"I see you are doing quite well."

"Indeed."

Both walk inside the house, the same house with the white picket fence and the stone side wall.

"Nothing has changed," says Susan, as she walks around the house.

"Very soon there will be."

"I'm waiting."

"Some tea?"

"Sure, why not for the last time?"

Alan pours two cups of tea and hands her one. He expresses how he will miss the city and that, for the first time, he's here to live on Long Island.

"I'll miss New York City and the bar."

"You could hop around every Friday."

"The due is still left unsaid."

"And what's that?"

"Why did you join the police?"

"You didn't forget, did you? Why don't you come over a beer, perhaps you could write a novel on that," Susan grins.

"Yes, Friday awaits," Alan nods, laughing with a jovial countenance.

As the Sun goes down, and the darkness reveals itself in the empty sky. Susan gets a call. Some tasks arrive at her door. *The City Mayor has been murdered in his residence,* she hears accurately. She bids a lasting farewell to Alan, drives her Chevy, speeds on the track, and vanishes for the new assignment.

Acknowledgments

I'm indebted to people who were associated with me throughout. My friends and family members are an integral part of this work. Without them, this work wouldn't have taken shape. I'm grateful to my publisher, who allows writers to have a platform and makes their voice heard globally.

To my dear sisters Bloomy Hajong, Ebica Hajong, and brother Econ Hajong, whose support played a significant role in building my confidence. My Parents, who are the vital part of all, need to be acknowledged for all the things they have done.

And my largest debt is to my late Grandmother, though she cannot read and write; her blessing to me in every walk of life is a gift. I'm highly grateful to her.

To my publisher, especially Nu Voice press of Hubhawks, who made it possible. Their support and work has reduced the effort and time conveniently.

About the Author

Beatone Hajong is an Indian Author who lives in the State of Meghalaya. After pursuing a degree in Engineering, he opted to go for writing, a passion that he wanted to explore, and authored two novels, *Side by Side*, *A Turn in the Road* which have received phenomenal reviews among global readers.

For more information and to know more about the author, you can connect with him on social media platforms.

Facebook: https://www.facebook.com/beatone.hajong.16/

Instagram: https://www.instagram.com/beatone_hajong/

Email: Writerbeatone@gmail.com

About the Author